Hunk of Burnin' Love

Hunk of Burnin' Love
by
Catherine Macleod

IMPORTANT COPYRIGHT NOTICE

First printed June 2019

All rights reserved. Copyright 2019
Content copyright © Catherine Macleod
Publisher copyright © Book Bubble Press

No part of this publication may be reproduced, distributed, stored in a retrieval system or transmitted in any form and at any time or by any means mechanical, electronic, photocopying, recording or otherwise, without the prior, written permission of the publisher.

The right of Catherine Macleod to be identified as the author of this work has been asserted by her in accordance with the Copyright, Design and Patents act 1988.
All characters in this publication are fictitious and any resemblance to real persons living or dead is purely coincidental.

A CIP record of this book is available from the British Library.

ISBN: 978-1-912494-42-2

Published in the United Kingdom by

Book Bubble Press

www.bookbubblepress.com

books@bookbubblepress.com

@bookbubblepress

Hunk of Burnin' Love

By Catherine Macleod

Book Bubble Press

Chapter
– One –

Take my breath away is singing in the background. My very own Tom Cruise is whisking me away into the sunset on the back of his Harley Davidson. Ahead fighter jets are diving through the sky. I can feel the power of their engines ripping through my whole body. It's exhilarating. My thighs are wrapped around his waist and I press my chest into this extraordinary man tightly. He smells mighty fine and so fresh; I could eat him right here. He turns and gives me that all American smile, wearing his aviator glasses. It makes me melt. I want him to pull over and ravish me underneath the air show, but he keeps on driving into the sunset. The warm wind wafts my hair back and the gentle breeze gives me a shudder. It's intoxicating. As the sun begins to disappear, the song concludes and he pulls over. He stops the bike and turns to face me.

My heart is pumping out of my rib-cage. He leans forwards and his lips gently touch mine and I am lost in this moment. "Ooh Tom...Ooh Tom" I moan. Looking around I blink a couple of times to see if I am wrapped around him? Instead, I am cuddling my enormous duvet and snuggling my Egyptian cotton pillow. Rolling over, I cry out loud! "Aww Nora Batty, it was just another dream!" I seem to live my life through blooming movies these days, or just dream about them. I try to get back to my dream. I squeeze my eyes shut tightly in an attempt to return to the dream and see Tom with his luscious chops. I try this for a good few minutes and then give up. I'm awake now and there is no return. Where is my happily ever after when it comes to a man? All these romantic scenes in movies should be available to hire. I'd love to step into one of the most famous movie scenes and take the place of the leading lady. Like that moment in Footloose (the original with Mr Bacon) when Ariel arrives on the porch all dressed up for the dance and he cannot muster any words due to the beauty that stands before him. I know that I would take the breath away of any man – especially in the morning rocking my Rod Stewart hair-do and sexy woolie bed socks.

When I watch movies and the ladies are dressed looking hot in their lacy numbers at bedtime I wonder if this is a true reflection of the women in real life? I really hope it isn't because I need my tartan pjs and thermal vest to snuggle into and cover up my wobbly bits. My wobbly bits actually look quite good when I am lying down. For now, I shall have to appreciate them for myself and nurture them.

My crisp, white bed sheets feel so good cocooned around my body – well something has to. I just love to snuggle any time of day really. I like a blanket to accompany me to most places, which makes me feel warm inside and out. The sun is currently beaming in through my wall of windows in my bedroom. It is warming me up and giving me a gentle wake up call. It dawns on me that it is the weekend and the start of my leave, so I can enjoy this leisurely stretch a little longer. This feeling is worth bottling – I'm sure I would make a bloody fortune! At this moment life is worth living; I have nobody nagging at me, no sense of dread and nothing to rush to. So, I fully intend to soak this up. Life rushes by so fast, I need to start enjoying it a bit more and realise how lucky I am. I may not have Tom Cruise by my side, but I can enjoy my own company. The fact is that I have to, as I am probably too good for him anyway – says the lonely woman in the sexy baggy pjs!

As I look through the window I feel so lucky about where I live. My apartment is on the coast of England and I can see the sea from where I lie in bed. Every day I wake to the sound of the waves and seagulls colliding together in harmony. Does that sound nice? Whether it's stormy or serine, it is my solitude and where I can be me. I live here alone, no children or adorning husband to love and cherish me. For the moment 'and I stress for the moment' I am happy with this – a girl needs to enjoy life before settling down and that is exactly what I will do (to the dismay of my mother). There must be one hunk of burnin' love out there for me? Surely there is at least one for everyone? I'm not that picky, I just require a number of things to make him perfecto. Have you ever seen the movie Weird Science? Well, firstly it is hilarious and secondly I wish I could make my own man – although I will avoid wearing my bra on my head... but maybe a jockstrap would work? What a sight that would be. On my 'find a man' wish list (which is in my head at all times) would be a number of things:-

1. An amazing smile which beams every time he sees me. There is just something about a man smiling at you and being genuinely pleased to see you, which makes me feel wanted and special. Sounds a bit sad now I have written this down. I do have men smiling at me...now and then but it is very rare. Everyone seems so busy now a days that they just don't have time to smile. Miserable gits I say!

2. Firm arms to embrace me and hold me close – I particularly like the muscle veins on the forearms. Not sure why and would probably sound odd if I said this out loud. So, I shall keep this to myself. They need to be strong enough to hold me up against the tiles in the shower and devour me under one of those rain fall shower heads. I don't ask for much and this is definitely on my rumpy wish list. I have a number of things on this list and if I am lucky the man of my dreams is reading this and will know what I want without the need to ask me. What is that I hear you shouting at me? Oh yes DREAM ON!

3. I also like my men tall, but not freakishly so. I'm only five foot four inches, so I don't want to look like a child next to him. Not a good look.

4. Hands, hands, hands – I don't want three pairs of hands (although now that's a thought hmmm). I always look at the hands. They need to be big, stocky (ish), trimmed nails with no werewolf hair protruding from anywhere. Gives me the hebbie-jebbies. Images of what these hands could do to me, own me and do naughty things to me wherever and whenever; makes me shiver with pure delight. Just a side note – I am a northern bird through and through so many of the sayings you may not have a clue about. I will try to remember this but just go with the flow and pick up some new vocabulary. Anyway back to the hands; I feel they were designed only for sheer pleasure and make me feel like a woman. I love it when men tickle the top of my leg it makes me feel woozy and giddy. I like to see if they can find my happy spot, not many can. There is still time and hope and of course my own wonderful hands!

As you will be hearing about my life from now on; I am sure you want to hear all about the love or lack of it up to the present date. To be honest, there isn't much to tell. In high school I had a few boyfriends. In my first year of high school I 'went out with' a boy in the fifth year. Not sure how this came about? When I say we went out together. We did no such thing as go anywhere together. I wrote to him and asked him questions about himself and he wrote back. More of a pen pal. Can't actually remember kissing him. He didn't live far from me and I used to take him some quality Avon aftershaves round to his house as gifts. I thought this was really bang on trend. I would never go in, but chat on his doorstep then go home. Then there was one lad in my same year, I only went out with him to get closer to his hot brother. I know that this sounds bad, but he soon caught onto this and one day he sent one of his friends over to dump me. I had it coming but I never got it on with his brother – such a shame he had really full snoggable lips and floppy hair; I would have loved to have twirled my fingers in.

I remember having the odd lip lock on the yard with the boys, but I would never take it too far. When we were in the final year the Common Room (where we chilled out during breaks) gossip would be rife with who had slept with whom. Even some of the hottest lads had got laid with some right mingers. I just didn't have it in me minger or not to give up my cherry at such a young age. My dad would have also hunted the lad down and given them a right beating. I loved hearing about others getting it on and listening to the juicy gossip of how and where, but never took it that far myself. I did have one boy in school that would send shivers down my back bone whenever I saw him. He was Matthew Hill. Boy, his smile was amazing. He was a footballer, very stocky shoulders and was good at everything. I am sure this guy is in every school. I laughed with him, took him on during hockey lessons and helped him during French lessons – which was the only subject he sucked at. But I was just in the friend zone and that was fine, because I got to spend a lot of time with him. Just not in the way I would have wanted. I still often think today what I would do if I saw him? I heard he had moved to New Zealand and married. I wonder who the lucky lady is? I really hope she is a normal person and he didn't fall in love with Wonder Woman. This somehow would make me feel so much better about his taste in women.

Just before I left high school I got entangled in a love triangle. Myself, Joe and Ana. Ana really did like Joe and Joe really liked me. I was not sure how I felt. I probably fancied Ana more! So one day I was sat on the field with Joe and said that the only way I am going to know if I truly liked him was if we had a snog. I could see Ana in the distance watching us, so it was a bit awkward. He thought this was a good idea and started to get a little closer to me on the grass. I was a bit unsure at this stage, if this was such a good idea? He licked what can only be described as his inflatable flaky lips and moved in. Thinking back now they really freaked me out and still make me quiver today. Why had I not noticed these before? So, by now my idea was totally backfiring on me and I had changed my mind. I did not let Joe know this and he lunged in with his big chops. I thought he may suck me right into oblivion, so I jerked out of the way. Which led to me head butting his glasses off his head and as he went to grab them mid-flight, he totally missed and went in for a boob grab instead. He started to laugh; now I am not sure what about? My boobs were a decent enough size then, but something about it made him chuckle. I stood up holding my bruised face where his bloody glasses had caught me and left him in his own little world. Later on, I heard rumours in the common room that Joe had got to a base with me and the lads jeered him on. I couldn't be arsed telling anyone, so left it at that. He got it on with Ana not long after; who then spread rumours about what his humongous lips had done to her lady parts and he was a god to the lads. Maybe I missed out on a real treat? We will never know.

I am really not entirely sure what happened at college. There were plenty of young rampant men, but I just wasn't bothered. I worked hard on my studies and then headed to work to earn extra cash. My aim was to learn to drive and get out of the area I was living. My part-time job was at Willards the book store. It seemed to be where the action was – if you were into books. I worked on the counter and stocking shelves with Daniel. He was handsomeish, only a little bit taller than myself with a few teenage spots, but a nice friendly smile. We would stock the shelves joking around and we would have our lunch together. The fun happened, when we both went into the back looking for stock it would get a bit heated. He would press his body against me as he was reaching for something. I would get a right sniff of his yum aftershave and probably an arm pit in my face. We would do some kind of rub against each other. It would do wild stuff to my hormones and then I would turn red and my breathing would increase beyond the norm. Never once did I pounce on him. I just enjoyed the contact between us. He would then carry on working on the shop floor in full knowledge that my brain was working overtime on what could happen in the stock room. That could be another book entirely on it's own. Passion between the stock or a wild night in the stock cupboard. It only ever got wild in my imagination and probably the best place for it to happen. I needed the job and the last thing I wanted was to get the sack for a fumble in the back. Mr Thompson the owner was a lovely, kind hearted man and that would be the last thing he needed to see. He'd be scarred for life, the poor bloke.

In my twenties well again not much to report on that matter. I went travelling with my best friend Jen. We headed to Thailand, Australia, North America and Europe. We both had nights where we had too much to drink and ended up with someone we had met in a bar.

They were normally just for one night, as when you have your beer goggles on many people appear very attractive. Then, the next morning you turn over and wonder what the hell you brought back with you? They may have thought the same about me. There were only a couple of times that we brought the same guy back and it was just a habit and we knew they were decent and would bog off once we got our itches scratched! The change in this pattern occurred in San Francisco when Jen met Dan. He travelled around different parts of the Californian coast with us and we were all friends at the start, but I noticed the way he looked at Jen. It was a look full of pure adoration and lust. Their friendship blossomed and they moved in together when we returned to England. Today they are married and have a beautiful daughter called Ava. Alas, this did not happen to me. I returned single, again to the dismay of my mother. She even made a comment that she would at least be happy if I returned with a lady boy of Bangkok in hand. Honestly, she just wants me to marry off, whereas all I hope for is a nice guy to spend my time with and enjoy similar interests.

Back to the present day where there is not much action going on. I'm normally on my fifth Porn Star Martini when I see a nice bloke. Try a sexy smile, which is more like I've had a stroke and pump out some good moves, which is more like a robot doing Hammer Time. Hence, no man heads in my direction. I actually scope a place out when I enter to judge who I am going to 'give the eye'. Have you heard that expression before? To give 'the eye' means that you look at someone to grab their attention then quickly look away. Then look like you are the most fascinating person in the venue, laugh and laugh some more. Then give them a quick glance again to see if they are still interested. If they are, I usually carry on with this performance and then head to the toilets hopefully heading their way and have a closer look. If they are not looking in my way at all then they get no more of my eye time and then I vouch to stop doing it. Until another hottie turns up, then my routine starts all over again. Then I vow not to do it again, but I do.

I'm 32, but have the musical knowledge of a 70 year old. The eclectic range of music comes from my nutty family. Ranging from Barry Manilow to Dire Straits. I have a real knack for remembering lyrics to songs – nothing else will stay in there – just songs! I'm useless at normal recall of say historical events, but I can burst out a Shawaddy Waddy tune. Bizarre I know, never ask me to join you on a quiz team unless it is related to song lyrics. You can find me at many points during my day listening to conversations and thinking about a song that links to it. For example in a conversation someone may say simply that this is crazy and I will carry on singing 'crazy for making me feel lonely' - in the words of Patsy Cline. People are used to me now and generally try to join in. Or just walk away from me.

In my apartment I can look out across the beach for miles and it always makes me feel calm and positive. When I head into the city for work I love the hustle and bustle, but definitely need this place to return to at night. My work friends always seem worried about me going home alone after work and they want me to stay at their apartment in the city. The fact of the matter is that I like my own company and enjoy the peace. Is that sad that I feel like this at 32? It is maybe why I can't find a good old man to bring me a nice brew in bed and warm my feet on during the night. By the way I hate cold feet! If my feet are cold I am the grumpiest bugger, so me and my bed socks rock the night away together. Oh boy I am not selling myself at all….a loner who loves bed socks. My future sounds bleak right there. I think I am just an old romantic – emphasis on the old.

I often sit on my balcony with a nice glass of wine and I imagine having romantic walks along the beach at dusk. This is my favourite time of the day; it makes my mood change into what one can only describe as a horny little minx. I think it's the light and a soft wind rippling in my hair which turns me on. Some days I try to re-enact this on my own, as I take a stroll down to the beach. I hold on to some hope that there is another man walking towards me doing the same.

In reality my hair turns into knots because the wind is wild and the sand is hitting me in the mush and romance has done a runner into the ocean. Not romantic or attractive. I do daydream a heck of a lot and life is much more romantic in my head than real life.

My phone starts to ring and startles my thoughts. The ringtone is the song Shut Up and Dance, which blares across my bedroom. I love this song and decide to shake my booty. It takes me a minute to realise that my mobile may need answering. Who the bloody Nora is wrecking my Saturday in bed? The nerve. I check to see if I can ignore it, but it is my friend Jenny. Mum of one, she has probably been up since the crack of dawn with her 2 year old daughter Ava. As I answer, Jen finds it hilarious to put Ava on the phone. I put it on speaker and lie back on the bed. Five minutes later, Jen decides to come on and speak to me. First thing she says is "I know it drives you insane, but I can't resist." Well ha bloody ha – why do it? I say to myself. I don't want to upset her, she is like a sister to me and has been through a lot with me. However, things like this do my head in!

"Are you up yet lazy bones?" Jen asks and knows the answer too, so I just grunt. "Well I have been up since 6am; done the ironing, put the slow cooker on and stripped the beds. Ava thinks it's party time at stupid o'clock, so I just go with it." Jen keeps going on about everything she has done, which can make me feel pretty useless. "You must appreciate this time to yourself

Emma. When I was single with no children, I had all the time in the world and it was wonderful. Guess what?" I just grunt..again. "I didn't appreciate it and no bugger told me to, so I am doing you a favour early on in life." She likes to tell me this every time she rings me at daft o'clock in the morning. "Why don't you have a man with you Em? You need to start getting some action or your bits will begin to shrivel up!" I lie there laughing, she does make me smile. But it is also very true.

"I'm just not meeting a man who I'd like to share my wobbly bits with." I put my face into my snuggly pillows and moan. I think I'm more worried that I don't fit any man's list or do I have that totally wrong? I wouldn't know, as the men I talk to are always drooling over somebody else. Jen is ruining my morning now as I am thinking too much about this. I say goodbye to my nutter of a friend, who has also slightly depressed me and plan to meet her at the beach bbq later on.

I'm debating whether to stay in bed, but looking outside it looks warm and some sunshine is needed on my pale skin. There are fit ladies already pounding the sand with their running gear on and looking mighty fine. I couldn't wear material like that which clings to your skin – boy I would end up looking like Chunk from the Goonies. What was it he did? The truffle shuffle? I can just picture the scene now and I would scare every living thing from the beach. I love seeing the sun, it makes me so much happier. Think I have been vitamin d deficient for some time living in this country. The lack of sun recently is depressing. As much as I don't want to start shredding the layers and showing more skin I have had enough of wearing jumpers. I head to my kitchen and search for a yummy breakfast to start my day. Cereal...toast...fruit. No nothing is tickling my fancy. So I decide to head out to Sam's Boat Yard for the best sausage butty in town.

Chapter
– Two –

Now before you read chapter two, make yourself a nice brew and a sausage butty (vegetarian or meat whichever you prefer) – sets the ambience for the boat yard.

As soon as I step out, the sun hits my skin and warms up my whole body. I definitely need to hit the beach soon and get my legs out for a bit of colour. They look like blooming corned beef legs or pale thorpe sausage legs i.e. pale and blotchy up North. Scare the seagulls away they will. At least I've had a shave and given them a treat. Nice to not shave over the winter months, but when you do they feel bloody cold. Like shaving a polar bear – I can really feel the cold now. I meander down towards the boat yard, just a five minute walk from my home. It is a hut next to a load of boats funny enough. It has the best views looking over the sea, where you can imagine sailing away with a hottie. Like in the movie

Jewel in the Nile, when Michael Douglas and Kathleen Turner sail around the world exploring and writing. That sounds like the perfect life, I just need to need to find a jewel to finance the venture. Looking around it looks quiet – it is early in the season so I can grab one of the tables near the beach edge. In the height of summer there is normally a queue around the building – I think tourists and locals get a whiff of the glorious sausage sandwiches early in the morning and they gravitate towards it. I'm never up early enough to beat the crowds, so I enjoy the time before the madness begins.

I hope James isn't working today. Butterflies fill my stomach every time we talk. He is too good looking for his own good and a nice guy. That combination is hard to find! Tall, blonde, tanned, muscles rippling through his white t-shirts, a smile which could crack anything open really. He part-owns this place with his twin brother Bobby. They set the boat yard shop up after their father died in a terrible boating accident two years ago. You never see James with a girl, he just seems to work and head out on his sail boat.

The death of his father, Sam really affected him and he does not talk about it to anyone. As I walk up to the counter, I feel relief to see his sister Polly working. She is in her early twenties, but is just as gorgeous and must have received the 'good looking' gene from the family.

"Morning." Poppy beams. "Will it be your usual?" She has such a great personality I bet men just come here to see her and the sausage butty is a bonus.

"Yes please and can I have a nice cup of English Breakfast too?"

"Sure thing Emma. Head over to your table and I will bring it over. Oh by the way how is your brother Tom doing? Haven't seen him around for some time." Poppy enquires.

"He's busy being a journalist in London. I haven't seen him that much either. Funny enough he is heading up to stay with me for a couple of days, you can catch up then." Is it just me or do I get the feeling that Poppy has a little soft spot for our Tom? When he sees how she has grown into this fine fetal of a woman, I think he will be eating sausage butties daily. Lord help him, I think she would eat him alive.

I head over to my table as a few more customers arrive. Poppy brings my tea over really fast and leaves me to enjoy the view. I sit looking out at the coast and forget all about work. Isn't it funny that when you see the sea, it has that magical touch and your worries seem to fade. The sky is lovely and blue – just the odd fluffy cloud bobbing around up there. There is a slight breeze, which gives me a little delightful shiver. Hugging my hot mug of tea, I can see boats bobbing around on the horizon. I often wonder who is on the boat? I normally come to the conclusion that it is a millionaire with his many ladies, sunning themselves whilst drinking champagne and having a dip in the water. They need to have Pitbull blasting out on their sound system and be wearing gold - barely covering a nipple- bikinis. I would be very disappointed if this was not the case.

My thoughts are interrupted by the vision that is James Dunn appearing beside me with my breakfast. An image of him doing this in the morning before I go to work hits my head. Wow. Then I realise he is talking to me, but I have no idea what he is saying. Everything seems to stop working when he is around.

"How do you stay so slim? You must go through a truck load of these each week? I'm surprised you actually don't look like a sausage sandwich by now." James laughs as he puts my food down in front of me.

I on the other hand nearly choke on fresh air, as James stands over me. Gordon Bennett this man is scrummy. I don't know what to say back, so I shove the sandwich in my mouth and take a huge bite. Bloody Nora it is hot, but I don't react because I will look more of a pillock. My eyes start to water and now I have chipmunk cheeks. Yes you have guessed it. I then start to talk – whilst eating. I know this is disgusting but something takes over my body in his presence and it is not pretty to watch. The wind hits me and he smells unbelievable. My body hardens and quivers with delight. The freshness from James taking a shower smell invades my nose and images of him taking that shower invade my head. I hum with pure satisfaction.

"You seem to be enjoying that today." James nods towards my food. Shit I totally forgot he was still stood there. Why is he still talking to me? It unnerves me. I giggle and look down at my t-shirt to see my two little peaks agreeing with him. I could have had his eyes out with them. So embarrassing! I just continue to nod. I'm scared now of him witnessing food between my teeth. If I hate one thing it is people not taking care of their nashers. I especially detest eating in front of someone and little black bits getting stuck between your canines. It is totally gross. I mean you'd hope someone would tell you, but on the other hand if they did I would just feel a knob. Like they are laughing and pointing at me shouting you..scrubber! "Are you heading to the bbq on the beach tonight?" James enquires. Shit, I had totally forgot he would be going.

"Yeah, I might. I do have a date though." I tease. Why have I just said that? I really do not have a date. However, James does appear uncomfortable, or is it my imagination?

"Oh, anyone I know?" he asks.

"Possibly not, they are Australian." I continue to munch away feeling happy and in control. The lies just continue to flood out. Shut your trap Emma.

"Okay, then hopefully see you and your Aussie later." James heads off to serve another group of pretty girls. Now I've lost the control. I am an idiot, why have I just told him I have a date? The only date I have planned is with a bottle of white Australian wine currently chilling in my fridge. Actually it is one of my favourite bottles, so it will be tough to choose...a bbq on the beach drooling over something I can't have Vs a cool Aussie on my veranda, something I can have! I love to have time to myself, but then I tend to think too much and this really hurts my brain. I will normally head to another of my movie scene fantasies and get totally swept away.

Watching James behind my sunglasses chatting animatedly to the customers, I realise he is just another Hollywood fantasy. It is not supposed to happen to me. I accept that; devour my butty and head home.

Chapter
- Three -

Getting ready for the beach bbq – now the question is do I go for comfort or slutty? For those that know me, they will be laughing at this comment. I don't have a slutty piece of clothing in my wardrobe. Something warm and comfortable it is then. Gone are the days of me wearing stupid heels or flesh revealing clothes. My common sense has found me, (unfortunately) or am I just turning into my mother? Scary thought. I am the one now who will make a comment on a night out about other girl's outfits. My concerns go along the lines of - how can she not have a coat on? Crikey she's got no tights on. Or does she know we are in October? I hate myself for this, but I still make silly comments and I'm only in my 30s. I've got my baggy hoodie on with leggings and my pumps. I give my long blonde hair a brush through and head out.

Heading down the path to the beach it's dusk outside. My favourite time of day (which you already know). I actually do feel very horny and confident at this time of day, as I strut along. I don't know what it is, but I feel the romance oozing from the amber coloured sky, the slight breeze wafting the trees and the quietness. It is warm and this makes me excited. Blimey I'm like a dog on heat. In the words of Paul Weller 'It does something to me, something deep inside!' It makes me shudder. As I stroll on I can faintly hear a guitar playing Oasis on the beach. I can't help but sing along as I head down. "She's Electric..."

I look around at the locals enjoying a good old catch up before the crazy tourist season begins. Everyone looks happy drinking beer in their bare feet enjoying this beautiful setting. I spy Jen talking with a group of men, thank goodness she is here. She is so confident talking to the other species, after all these years I still haven't worked out how she does it. She is a natural. She spots me, smiles and heads over.

"I didn't think you'd make it." Jen laughs as she gives me an enormous cuddle.

"I know what you're like Emma when you have bought a good bottle of plonk and some nibbles." This comment makes me laugh out loud, this girl knows me so well.

"Jen you still have a way with the men. I could see them hanging on your every word. You must have a secret?" I nudge her. "Come on Jen, give it up. You know I am in need of advice in any shape or form. My lady bits are beginning to shrivel up, with the lack of attention. Desperate times and all that." Jen nearly chokes on her beer.

"Come on Em, that is not a nice image that you have put into my head." Jen shakes her finger at me in disgust.

"Do you really want to know?" Jen asks me. I nod very enthusiastically waiting for the words, which are going to change my world and get me laid. "I am happily married, so basically I could not give a toohoots what they think of me." Jen shares in a very matter of fact way. "So, I don't care what actually comes out of my mouth or if I talk to them with a mouth full of food, then so be it. They can take me as they find me and that my lovely friend is that." I try to digest this new information and make it work for me.

"So you don't care what they think, which actually makes them like you more?" I ask looking puzzled.

"Yes, now come on and show these men that you are worth the attention." Jen pushes me towards the bbq area.

Oh boy, I spot James cooking away on the fire, wearing a t-shirt which emphasises all his wonderful muscles. Holy moly guacamole, he is just mighty fine. With the Transvision Vamp 'baby I don't care' lyrics pumping in my head, I walk over towards him. He is sipping a bottle of Brooklyn and tending to the meat on the grill with skill. He spots me spying on him and I blush crimson red feeling a total idiot. I only saw him this morning and I feel like I am at high school again, pathetic. He mouths something at me, but I haven't a clue, so I hold my beer up to cheers him and move away hoping the sand soaks me up.

Jen has now left me and continues to work her way around the crowd engaging in talk with ease. Come on Emma, I say to myself you can do this. I carry on singing to myself 'I I I I I don't care.....' I need to be more like Jen and stop searching for a decent man to take notice of me. Surely there is one out there and we will meet. Soon. I hope.

I mooch around the fire and find a deck chair, a cosy blanket and grab a nice cold bottle of Big Wave from the beer bucket. I begin talking to some old school friends, who I have known for years. It is nice to catch up and it doesn't matter how long it has been since we have seen each other, we talk like we saw each other yesterday. So easy and relaxed. Amy, one of my oldest friends in the area, starts to reminisce about our crushes at high school.
"Do you remember Mr Green our music teacher?" she asks me. "Boy you had a crush on him." This was directed right at me.
"No I didn't." I exclaim in shock.
"Of course you did. You would get into trouble just to spend detention with him." She sits back in her deck chair laughing. I try to remember if this was actually true, the older I get the more I forget, or want to forget.
"I think he actually quite liked you too Emma." She squeals with her eye brows raised.

"No way" I shout, spraying out my beer. "I'm sure if we saw him today, we would wonder what all the fuss was about? It's just high school hormones Amy. They were rife."

"Sure was babes and probably still is today. Don't think I would survive now at high school, they seem so much taller and more grown up from when we went. Now, I need a top up- do you want anything Emma?" I can't help but laugh at my old friend, as she tries to push herself up from the deck chair, wine glass in hand and failing miserably. I help her up and she stumbles a little and falls right back.

"Think you need to head to the old folks home down the road Amy." James comments as he helps her up from the chair.

"Cheeky bugger, well if I am going you can all join me too. Mr Green is probably already in there Emma, so I will send him your love!" Amy heads off into the darkness. Not sure if she has her own stash of wine hidden in the dunes or she really has had too much to drink and doesn't know where she is going. James sits himself down next to me and takes a part of my blanket to cover himself.

"Do you think we should go and find her and see where she is going?" I ask James looking over to where Amy had just disappeared to. He starts to look around and points over to Jen.

"Looks like your BFF has found her."

Amy is now hugging onto Jen and dribbling on her shoulder and she plonks her down on the sand near a group of locals. She waves over to us and gives us the thumbs up, so that they are both okay. Jen to the rescue! I look back at James whose chiselled cheek bones are so defined by the light of the fire. His eyes are twinkling away and I get that all familiar feeling down below that drives my hormones crazy. This town is missing a great deal of talent, but this man before me has it in his finger tips – or is it just the 4 bottles of Pinot I demolished before heading down? I look over to Jen, who knows exactly what is going on in my head and body. She mimics 'deep breaths'. This brings a smile to my face and I start to give it a go, but as I am doing it I realise that I look like I am about to give birth.

"Are you okay Emma?" James asks looking at with me with clear confusion on his face as to why Chewbacca is at the side of him. How is it the brain and mouth do not engage when you are talking to someone you like?

I try to think of something to say back, but my brain has gone to sleep zzzzzzzzzzzzzzzzzzzzzzzzzzzzzzzz

All I can do is just nod like the bloody Churchill dog and take a big gulp of my beer. No wonder I am single – can't even listen and respond. A simple task a five year old could do.

"I thought you had a date with a hot Aussie?" James asks.

"Oh yes, I have already met with the scrummy Aussie." I reply with a smirk. I am going to let this joke last a little longer.

"What is his name?" he asks. Is he asking because he is just making conversation or is there more to his questioning?

"It is an unusual name really." I express "He is called Wolf and he was very chilled indeed. I enjoyed a little of his company, then headed down here." I explain.

"That really is different, did he not fancy joining you?" he asks.

"No I have binned the Aussie and I am now in the mood for a good old French one next." I begin to giggle.

"Blimey Emma, you treat them mean. Didn't realise you were like that." James shakes his head looking a little concerned at me.

"Well, how do you treat a bottle of wine?" I respond looking at his confused face. I then see the truth dawn on him and he gives out a good chortle. We sit back in our deck chairs, laughing.

"You really had me going there Emma. That was very clever about Wolf you meant Wolf Blast the wine. Ha. I knew deep down that you wouldn't have a man up there. You are just like me; you enjoy your own company." James looks at me sheepish like he has said something out of turn. I just nod and look back at the fire. Do I really just like my own company or do I want a man in my life? His comment has made me question myself a little. It is not good to be doing any deep thinking when you have consumed so much alcohol, so I just shrug it off.

"Did I say something wrong Emma?" James enquires looking at me a little worried.

"No, not at all." I say looking quickly back at the smouldering fire in front of us.

James' brother Bobby is getting everyone singing along as he plays some great tunes on his guitar. Jenny comes back over and snuggles up next to me – her cheeks are rosy red hot from the camp fire and the many drinky poos she has enjoyed. We are all signing along to Reef's Put your hands on and I just can't help myself – I need to dance. This song takes me back to being younger, it is such a tune. It really is not easy dancing on sand and I probably look a right plonker, but it must be the beer, because I don't care. I go into my own little world and when I open my eyes more people have joined me. I just love this place.

As Bobby continues to play I feel like I am getting a bit sweaty and decide to walk a little away from the party, so I take a stroll along the beach. I find a lovely spot not too far away from everyone but I feel the peace very calming and a cool breeze is starting to hit my body. That is so much better. I need to calm down now. I lie back on the sand, which is also cold against my warm skin. I look up at the stars. There are so many to see. I have no idea what their real names are, I just make them up for my own constellation. I begin to think back to one of my favourite childhood movies, Jaws. In the opening scene there is a young lad on the beach lying there wasted, whilst a girl he likes is being a nice tasty supper for the big bugger of a shark in the ocean. Freaks me out to think what could be lurking beneath those waves at night. What if something is watching me right now? It makes me shudder.

"I've been watching you" whispers James in my ear.

"Oh my word." I shriek.

"I was just thinking about something in the sea doing the very same thing and between you and me I nearly wet myself thanks very much." I ramble as I slap his arm.

Laughing James lies next to me on the sand.

"You are such a curious creature" he says whilst moving very close to me. "What are you doing over here alone?" he asks.

I point to the stars in the sky and for some reason I start to share with him my names for my own constellation.

"Well, over here you can see a cluster of stars and this is called a chip butty – one of my favourite things to eat, well apart from your sausage baps. Over here you can see the mighty Thor – my favourite Avenger." As I explain my crazy star system he does not joke or make fun of me. He just listens as I continue to share my constellation system with him. He starts to smile as I talk and his fingers begin to gently touch my own in the sand beside me. This is nice and something I would normally retract from, but I like it. My mother always says 'a little of what you fancy does you good' well bring it on I say. He turns on his side to get even closer to me. This is making me nervous. His fingers begin to trace along my arm. Holy moly this is such a nice moment and it is making all my hairs stand to attention. My brain is telling me to stop this from happening right now. I do not want to lead this poor bloke on. My groin on the other hand is waking up from a deep sleep and is beginning to purr. A frolic in the sand is just what I need. I am really enjoying his touch, so I leave him to it, close my eyes and remain lying there.

"Emma, wake up!" Jen startles me awake. I look around and I'm alone still lying on the sand. Ahead the party has died down and people are leaving.
"Em, you fell asleep. Come on, let's get you home drunken bum." Jen laughs as she pulls me up off the sand.

"Where has James gone?" I ask "One minute he is ...well…being very nice, the next…"

"You fell asleep on him and did a huge beer burp. At which point he came to find me." Jen explains. The look on my face says it all.

"Oh no I didn't. You have got to be kidding me? Is that what he told you? Oh boy I am disgusting." I shake Jen for the truth.

"I am afraid so, you're such a catch Em." Jen begins to really laugh, which makes me do too. In fact I laugh so much it hurts my stomach as we walk back to my place. I have to see the funny side of it or it would really upset me. Which man would stick around knowing that I do things like that? I really am gross.

Chapter
- Four -

I try to open my eyes, but they are so sore and my tongue is sticking to the roof of my mouth. In fact I can hardly open my mouth. My brother would say that this is a brucey bonus as I do tend to talk a lot. I try again to open my eyes, but they are stinging and are refusing to budge. I start to panic a little about what happened last night. Where did I end up? I really cannot remember. I decide for my own safety I need to slowly take a peek at where I am actually lying. I open the left eye slowly, this is painful. The light in this place is off the bloody scale, it is so bright who would be crazy enough to live like this? I can see a blur of a bedside lamp and a stack of familiar novels at the side of it. Oh thank heavens I am home. Not sure how I made it here, but I am very thankful. On another note I must sort out the lighting in here – too much of it going on for my liking. What was I thinking? Knowing I am home and safe I have a contented groan and turn over in my bed. I feel as rough as a bear's arse today, so I think a day in bed is in order. I take hold of my pillow for a snuggle and realise that what I am actually touching does not feel like a pillow. What the hell am I touching? As I try to open both eyes in total bloody fear they start to water. The light in here is totally shit! I continue to have a feel around me and this time it moves. Holy moly what the blooming Nora was that? Did I bring a man back? Who though? Totally out of character for me. I hear a moan, so I leap out of bed armed with one of my novels.

"Back off moving thing. I am armed with a Deaver." I screech and try to open one eye again.

"Emma what are you doing, you nutter?" a lady's voice squeaks at me, sounding quite alarmed.

"Jen?" I enquire pulling my eye lids right back to see her.

"Yes of course it is me, now put down Mr Deaver before there is another crime to write about" grumbles Jen quite annoyed.

"Did you stay over?" I ask.

"Yes, well obviously. I wasn't leaving you, the state you were in" Jen answers getting more annoyed with me.

"Oh thank you. You are such a good friend. I don't deserve you." I jump back into bed and give her a squeeze. She snuggles in, so I know she has forgiven me.

"Crickey Em you do have dog breath." She giggles and pushes me away. I blow my breath into my hand and yes she is right, woohoo that is bad. Another disgusting trait to add to the list of mine. ERR!

"Sorry Jen, I don't think I brushed my teeth last night." I explain as the smell actually knocks me sick. "In fact I don't think anything got a clean last night." I look down my body to see that I'm still in the clothes that I went to the beach bbq in. I look like I have been dragged over a sand dune a couple of times. No wonder I am alone. If any man had woken up to this sorry state of a woman, I think I'd put him off women for life.

"Come here my lovely, nutter of a friend." Jen opens her arms for another cuddle. "At least one thing I am sure of is that James had his eye on you last night." She states with a grin. I raise my eyebrows in the 'are you kidding?' kind of way. "Yep" she continues "I have not seen James like that for some time. However, after your snoring antics, I'm not sure we will again!" Jen pushes me away laughing and I grab my pillow to hide the shame on my face. The poor bloke.

I try to recall the night, but my brain is hurting. "I think we were talking about the stars and the movie Jaws. Oh yes I told him about my own constellation. Not sure what he thought about that? I remember he was rubbing my arm – oh boy it was so nice. Got my nipples rock hard." We roll into each other laughing. It hurt so much to laugh. My rib cage was not happy jiggling about. I really was a pillock last night, but to be fair, whoever ends up with me will have to love that about me. There is no changing this old bird! The pounding in my poorly head begins to worsen. I need painkillers and more sleep. I'm not a doctor but I think that is a damn good prescription.

"Do you fancy some breakfast?" Jen asks as she climbs out of bed.

"Oh yes, if you are up to it? Let me know if you need any help. I will be right here." I shout to her as she enters the kitchen. I turn over, spread my whole body out and snuggle back up.

I must have fallen back to sleep, I am a bit disorientated when I awake. I can hear Jen shouting me- she must have poured the cornflakes into a bowl by now for me. Bless her, she's a gem. I sit myself up in bed, but my head feels like bloody lead and I fall back onto the duvet. I hate having a hangover. Why do I do it to myself? I am rubbish at looking after myself after a session on the booze.

"Come on Emma, get your butt out of bed. I have made you something good!" Shouts Jen rather too energetically.

I groan but pull myself up again. Wobbling a bit now I head in the direction of the amazing smell. "Hey, bossy. You're not at home now. Be nice, I'm delicate," I plead. But Jen has been cooking, so I try to move that bit faster. I am so excited someone has cooked me breakfast. As I'm passing my bedroom mirror I catch a glimpse of myself. Crickey, I look old. My hair is wild. My eyes are like piss holes in the snow. My skin looks, well, just shit frankly. No other way of putting it. Rough as! Sod it. The smell then takes over my body and I float towards Jen. Luckily, Jen has seen me like this on many occasions, so I do not worry about what she thinks of her oldest and not so wisest friend.

As I enter the kitchen, my table is set for two, with fresh juice and a nice pot of tea. I sit down and Jen places a full English brekkie in front of me. Oh yes, this is what the doctor ordered – a grease fest to soak up all the alcohol consumed last night.

"Have I ever told you Jen, that you are the bestest friend on the planet and I love you very much?" I gush on as I shovel eggs, beans and mushrooms into my mouth all at once.

"I think it is truly needed today Em. Hopefully, it will make you feel better." Jen replies as she finishes plating her own breakfast. She walks over to join me in a right jolly old mood singing away to Charles and Eddie on the radio.

"I do love this song" she adds whilst singing "would I lie to you baby..oh yeah!" I have no choice but to join in. It is such a classic. "I'm telling you baby you will never find another soul with this heart of mine...oooh ooohh" we continue together munching and singing together.

At times pretending the toast or sausages are our microphones. We are pretty on point if I may say so. This moment takes me back to university, when we would just put Whitney Houston tunes on and sing away to the lyrics, whilst polishing off a bottle of wine or four. I especially loved our rendition of Queen of the Night. We would add actions taken from the Bodyguard movie and pretend Kevin Costner was in our audience. Nothing much has changed with us to be fair. We still do have nights like this.

Jen looks so fresh sat in front of me. Her brown bobbed hair has a natural wavy kink and just looks chic. Her blue eyes are twinkling and her skin has that dewy fresh look about it. She is so natural.
"How do you do it?" I ask her. "How do you look so good after polishing off a lot of booze last night?" I ask hoping for a magic answer.
"I stay on beer and drink water in between. I can't add wine to the mix, as that would make a girl a bit loopy...like yourself" she explains laughing. "After Ava was born I just couldn't handle my alcohol like I used to. I also couldn't handle a hangover when the little monkey

woke up at 5 sodding o'clock in the morning." She explains whilst chewing on her bacon. She can't half eat as well – nothing to her 5"5 frame. I can only assume that she has a really massive big toe where it all goes!

"So Em, what do you have planned for the rest of the day?" Jen asks me.

"Tom is coming up from London tomorrow, so I need to have a bit of a clean-up and sort somewhere for him to sleep. I have taken a few days off work to spend with him." As I am telling Jen I am looking around at the place and taking in the thick layers of dust surrounding me. "I think it could do with a little TLC – hasn't seen a duster or hoover for some time. How are you fixed for helping with that?" I ask Jen but I already know the answer.

"Not a bloody chance, after this I am heading home to my family and taking Ava to her swimming class. She loves it and I enjoy sitting on a deck chair by the side of the pool having a brew and eyeing up the coaches. Highlight of my week" Jen shares smiling away at the happy thought. "That is until my little girl begins to waste a good lesson by messing about." Jen starts to look annoyed whilst finishing her food. "I try to tell her off with my eye brows, a shake of the head, a wagging of my finger. But then she shouts across the pool – what's up mummy? So at this point I get a stern look from the coach for interrupting the lesson and I can hear hooty tooty other parents tutting. So I can't bloody win."

"I can take her one week. Happy to help if it stresses you out so much." I offer whilst taking a nice big sip of my tea. I've never really seen Jen get worked up about anything really. She is a very chilled lady – but I can tell this really frustrates her. The effect of having kids I'd expect and the effect they can have on your mental state.

"Ha, you just heard that I eye the coaches up and fancy a bit for yourself." Jen states raising her trimmed eye brows at me. I watch her and she is eating really fast – another effect of having children, eat whilst you can. It is starting to make me feel a little woozy, so I stop watching her.

"Easy tiger, slow down" I say to Jen as she runs the remaining piece of toast over her breakfast juices.

"Sorry Em, I've got to head off." Jen replies as she starts to clear her plate away. She walks over to me plants a kiss on my head and heads towards the door. "Enjoy your afternoon cleaning Em and I will give you a ring later." I carrying on scoffing and wave her away.

"Thanks for looking after this old codger. I'm sure to return the favour...maybe one day." I say giggling knowing full well that will never happen.

"Say hi to your brother for me. Bring him over Monday night. I am having a few friends bobbing round and it'll be nice to catch up." Jen waves as she goes through my front door.

Looking down at my plate I still have a lot to eat but I start to feel sick. So sick. I think the eggs are ready to pop back up to say hello. I launch myself into the bathroom and start to hug my toilet. As I'm kneeling there it occurs to me that I am actually an idiot and 30 something's don't act like this anymore. I really need to get my act together. I hug my stomach and lie down on the floor beside the toilet. Bloody Nora it is disgusting down here, loads of bloody cobwebs and dead insects. This needs to be first on my scrub list. But cleaning is not immediately on my agenda. I have the overwhelming feeling to just close my eyes for a minute and everything will be okay in the world.

My eyes are closed. He touches my neck, then gently tickles my cheek. I can hear him breathing deeply beside me and it ignites the giddy hormones in my body. I slowly open my eyes to see Josh Hartnett looking down at me with his big beautiful eyes. He is in my home and holding a flower over me. I am lying on my living room carpet with candles flickering around me. I begin to talk and he presses his finger on my lips to quieten me. He then continues to move the flower teasingly to different parts of my body..my chest following down to my naval and heading to my sweet spot. Holy moly, how can he have this affect on me with a blooming flower? I can feel his chest rising up and down rapidly beside me and I can tell he is excited too. Do I dive on him now? Or do I let the tension build? I squeeze my eyes tightly and enjoy this. But there is something wrong, I don't feel right. Hang on, what is that feeling between my thighs? Something is burning and I don't mean hot like sexy. I start to itch all over my body. My thighs are on fire and not with glee. I look down on my body and see that I am covered in stinging nettles. I sit up quickly to brush them all away. "SHIIIITTTTT" I yell. As I dive up I head butt the bleeding toilet seat. This launches me backwards towards my carpet. Hugging my bashed and poorly head I realise I must have fallen asleep on the toilet floor. I touch my body just to check that I am okay. No itching, no need to go and hunt down a bloody dock leaf. Do they actually work anyway? Or was it just something my mum would tell me to shut up. Psychological stuff! Looking on the floor I had actually made myself comfy. I had pulled down the towels from the radiator and made a little nest for myself with all the other dead insects. Nice.

Miraculously, I don't feel sick anymore and decide to head back to bed for a few more minutes. I touch my head and try to soothe the pain from bashing it. I notice on the clock that it is midday and I have probably slept on my toilet floor for about three bloody hours. I look at myself in the bedroom mirror and make a 'oh lordy lordy' sigh. I have toilet carpet patterns planted across my face. These will take hours to go away. It's a good job I am not going anywhere. You could add a bit of glitter to my patterns and I would be festival ready. My body still feels like lead and it is welcome relief to jump back amongst my covers and spread eagle right across.

Chapter
– Five –

Just a note that now would be a good time to pump up the American Anthems tunes for this chapter and this should get you in the mood for a spot of cleaning on your own place.

After a mighty cold shower to waken me up and a fresh mug of rosielea. I pop my sweats on and pull out my cleaning gear. It is time to get scrubbing my apartment. I just love to clean to music and I also class it as a good workout. The tune Maniac bursts on the radio, so I pump this right up. Grab my duster and start to shake it and dust. I get into a rhythm quite quickly and get the living room dusted in no time. Dancing was good enough for the Shake 'N' Vac girl, so why not put some freshness back into my apartment? Although, I do find it hard to clean during the choruses, as I tend to want to stop and boogie. If a crap tune comes on then that's when I do a spot of hoovering. I have it all planned in my head (very sad really) and it is a little routine of mine. I clean when I am stressed as well, as I feel it is a good strategy to let off steam and do something proactive at the same time. Didn't realise that when you picked this book there would be top tips did you? You are welcome.

I start to clean the TV, which is one of the worst jobs. I just can't do it without creating almighty shocking streaks. I try to dab at the screen in the hope that I can only make a small mess. My mum would freak if she saw it or even watched me attempt to clean it. She would say something along the lines of 'you do not possess the skills of a future wife.' Then after some time attempting to make it look reasonably watchable I say sod it and end up watching a smudgy Poldark. By the way he still looks hot smudgy on horseback!

The next song just stops me completely in my tracks. This is my song. It's about my life. Now this song deserves my full attention
"White skin on linen

Perfume on my wrists"

I grab the hoover pole as my microphone and give it some wellie.

"These dreams go on when I close my eyes

Every second of the night I live another life

These dreams that sleep when it's cold outside

Every moment I'm awake the further I'm away"

Do you know the feeling when you get so engrossed in singing a song you know so well, but help you if anyone heard you singing it? Well this is totally me singing this song. Like a cat being humped during the night i.e. scary! I just get carried away with the lyrics as I relate to them freakishly so. I get so engrossed in fact that I nearly choke on snorting hoover dust up my nostrils. A little bit of splurting and I'm all good to continue my solo. "This song is AMAZING!" I scream to my neighbours.

"These dreams go on when I close my eyes

Every second of the night I live another life

These dreams that sleep when it's cold outside

Every moment I'm awake the further I'm away"

I shimmer over to my lamp and dance around it. Just like I am back in my bedroom at my mum and dad's home. Ahhh the sweet memories. I can still remember making the ceiling shake with my dance moves and my dad shouting at me to cut it out or I'd be paying for new light fittings. Suffice to say I carried on. Actually, talking to my dad about it now just makes him smile. I think he quite enjoyed listening to me making up my own moves to songs. I sweep my duster over the lamp in an attempt to do a little more cleaning.

"Is it cloak 'n' dagger

Could it Spring or Fall?"

This song is just about me – living my life through dreams. The writer obviously understands that feeling too, hence I am not alone in the world after all. This is it now the conclusion. So much energy and emotion. I give it more power. Close my eyes and I jump off the sofa to belt out my grand finale. I spin and spin and twizzle my body around and land directly in front of "ARGHHHH. Who the hell are you?" I scream. There's a bloke..a real bloke in my home. At this point I totally freak. Raise my duster polish and spray the intruder directly in the eye balls. Launch the duster at him – which sticks to his face. Then I scream 'fire' at the top of my lungs. I know to shout this as my teacher told me so in my self-defence classes, as everyone reacts to a fire.

"Emma, I can't see. Emma I need some water. Shit this is stinging. Emma!"

He knows my name? His voice is also recognisable. I peer out from round the curtains (my hiding place of course) and take a peek at duster boy. Holy crap it is James! I have blinded poor James. I run over to him apologetically.

"James, I'm so sorry. I didn't recognise you in a baseball cap. I thought you were a burglar." I try to explain.

"Shit, Emma my eyes..." James reaches out and grabs me as I approach him and we both collide together. Crikey we are fumbling each other and hands are touching each other in many places! Our faces are very close together as we land on the sofa. He is very close to me and I feel a very warm feeling inside. This feeling does not sit right with me, so I rise quickly and shake away any fantasies that might be trying to pop into my head.

"Just sit here James, I will go and fetch a bowl of water for you to rinse your face. Don't move." I plead as a sprint towards the kitchen with images of me kissing him in my head.

"No bloody chance of me moving Emma. I can't see feck all!" James replies as I head into the kitchen. I've never heard James mad before. I return with a bowl and flannel. James gives his face and his eyes a good clean and I continue to apologise for spraying him.

"I'm so sorry James, I don't have men just turning up. Or wanting to see me for that matter." I explain.

"I wasn't here to see you, your brother invited me." James says matter of factly.

"Oh, I see." I say feeling a little deflated about this. "How long were you stood there for?" I ask not really wanting to know the answer.

"Long enough. I got a glimpse at yet another side of you Emma. Very nice pirouette on the rug by the way." He pokes my arm and smiles.

I put my face in my hands. "It's the only way I can clean. I need music to get me through it." I reply looking through my fingers horrified.

"Emma, I've got to be honest I did not see any cleaning going on. You looked well into the performance of a lifetime. But may I suggest you have a style team on hand before you go public." James looks me up and down. I take a brief look at myself and sigh. My hair is scraped right back on the top of my head – should have at least run some dry shampoo through it. My Take That t-shirt has paint on it from decorating and my jogging pants look like they belong to Vanilla Ice and emphasise all my wobbly bits around my tummy. Thank goodness my mum cannot see this. All I can hear is 'presentation at all times Emma'. Yes I look like a prick and James knows it. Then it dawns on me that I am allowed to do this kind of stuff in my own apartment and wear whatever the bloody Nora I fancy. I start to get defensive.

"James did you break and enter my property? Do I need to alert the neighbourhood watch team that there is a pervert on the loose?" I ask.

"Pervert? Do I look like one? Scrap that, don't answer it. I actually walked up to your door to knock and it was already open. I shouted many times, but you couldn't hear me as you were auditioning for The Voice." James explains in quite an angry tone. His eyes are really red and blood shocked, so he is looking pretty wild at this point.

"I don't understand. Jen must not have locked it when she left." I mutter. Thinking back though, I have been back to bed since she left and I would have been lying there with no clue that my door was open. I feel sick at the thought, but don't share any of this information with James. Boy, I live in a bloody safe place or the burglar or attacker did come in, saw the state of me and said sod this for a game of soldiers then legged it.

"So when does your brother arrive?" James asks.

"Oh Tom arrives tomorrow morning – hence why I am cleaning. Or at least trying to clean." I stifle a smile.

"Well I think my eyes are very shiny now and won't need another clean until next spring." James replies with a cracking smile, obviously trying to cheer me up and clear the air.

"Shall we have a brew? I feel like I need to make it up to you. I do have some lovely ginger nuts in, so we can have a dunk." I ask in hope he will say yes.

"Go on then Emma that sounds great." As James says this he nudges a little closer to me on the sofa. "However, it will take more than a brew and some ginger nuts to forgive the fact you nearly blinded me. I shall have a think and let you know when the time is

right." As James says this my mouth drops open and I just stare at him dumfounded. Is he being seductive? To me? I shift backwards, as I am really not sure how to react to this comment. So I jump up, yet again to escape the close proximity. I head and put the kettle on and find some nice mugs for us to use. Whilst I am in the kitchen I think back to my childhood and when we first met. We went to different schools, but lived across the road from each other. Our families used to get together regularly at each other's homes, normally so our parents could have a few beers and a chat. He is the same age as my brother, so they would be together most of the time after school. Tom didn't like me hanging around, so I would just look and admire from afar. James has never changed – all the guys want to be him and all the girls want to do him! He is someone that you want to be horrible, so it easier when he shrugs you off, but he is really nice. I mean really lovely to everyone. I shout through to James just to check that he is real and that he hasn't done a runner.
"I have another apology to make to you."

I peer around the door to see him standing looking out of my window at the sea. Sweet mama even from the back he is just too hot to handle. His fine buttocks are just as firm as a rock cake and his broad shoulders could take on Iron Man. He turns around and I shimmy back into the kitchen taking deep breaths as all these emotions wriggle inside me. A little more composed I head back in.

"Here we go." I say as I place the steaming hot mugs of builder's tea on the table. I sit beside him on the sofa, but a good space that I don't get any more crazy bleeding ideas. Thou shalt keep ones hands and lips to one's self.

"You said you had another apology? Does that mean my favour has just got bigger?" James asks with a cheeky smile.

"Well, I don't know about that! But I just want to say that I am sorry for falling asleep last night on the beach." I shovel a biscuit quickly into my mouth, just encase I say any more.

"I was very impressed with your constellation system. Especially, the mighty Thor. I think that one was my favourite." James places his hands on his hips as if he was Thor. Thank goodness he cannot read my mind, because I have him dressed in a toga with the wind blowing in his hair. A little bit of sweat and dirt on him from a battle with Thanos, where he rescued me from his evil clutches. James interrupts my thoughts. "I didn't mean to bore you. One minute we were chatting and the next you were dribbling or was it burping?" I squirm at the thought – not a pretty sight. I remember him tickling my arm and this sent me into another fantasy. It was so nice, I still get goose bumps thinking about it now. If only he knew that it wasn't just my face that was dribbling last night..ha!

"I just had a bit too much to drink and my hero Jen took care of me." I say sounding like a child. This is certainly a habit I need to stop and I need to start to manage my drink and think about the consequences. Now where the hell did that thought just come from? BBRRRR I do a shudder. I think I am actually growing up and my mum is doing a dance somewhere in her coffee shop. "Jen is having a few friends around at hers on Monday evening, pop round. I'm taking Tom with me. You two can catch up there." I add hoping he will say yes.

"Thanks for the offer, but I think I may be on a late shift at the boat yard. If I can change it, I will stop by." James replies whilst dunking his biscuit. "I'm looking forward to seeing old Tom. It's been a while and I am in the need of a good night out with him. He always knew how to wooe the ladies. I want some good tips." As James says this I spit out my tea. Gross Emma - why do I do things that are so unattractive?

"Did you say, you need help? Are you talking about the same James that I have known since I was 6 years old? The same James that girls gravitate to?" I ask shocked at his comment.

"Gravitate? More like float away from. I've been on a few dates, but nothing serious. I've put my heart into making the business a success after my dad passed away. Had no time for anything else. Think it's time I started to put some effort into finding a nice lady to look after me." He says in a teasing tone.

"Well, I do have one tip for you. Don't sneak up on anyone in their home. This not only freaks us ladies out, but we are armed with deadly polish and dust busters!" I say laughing as I finish my brew.

"Yes, good tip. Especially if they are in the middle of doing a rendition of Heart's Dreams. I shall consider myself warned." James adds. Wow, he knows the song I was singing. This only makes him go up in my estimation. This guy is a keeper. Does he have a bad side at all? I am not sure. It makes me wonder. "Well I better head off. Thanks Emma for giving my face a spring clean and the cuppa. Hope I can make it to Jen's on Monday. If not I'd quite like to catch up again soon...only if you'd like too?" James asks quite shyly.

"Oh..you mean you have seen me dribbling, seen me in my worst gear dancing to trashy songs and you would like to spend more time with me?" I asked confused.

"Yes." He answers simply.

"I'd like that too." I answer just as simply. We stand opposite each other just smiling.

The atmosphere just got very electric and I don't need anything else to make my hair wilder, so I show him straight to the door. James turns around suddenly.

"Emma, can you do me one thing?" James asks.

"What is it?" I ask in hope that he says 'just kiss my head off'.

"Please lock your door now. I don't know if another man's heart could take you tackling the American hits and their eyes certainly wouldn't survive the polish attack." He smiles and heads through the door. As he leaves I close the door and sit behind it. Oh my goodness that has just happened. To me.

Chapter
- Six -

I walk onto the train platform and keep a look out for my older brother, Tom. I'm so looking forward to seeing him. Standing on my tip toes I try to look over the crowd of tourists arriving at the station for their short breaks. I can see a group of ladies looking over at something that has caught their eye. As I follow their line of sight I can see they are all staring at Tom. He has just helped a lady with a pram off the train and they are all looking on wishing he would look their way. Tom is totally oblivious to this – always has been. At that point he notices me and shouts across the platform. He just looks like Clarke Kent – glasses and all. The only difference is, Tom cannot fly and does not wear underpants outside of his outfit. He is my hero though and his face is a happy sight. I run over to greet him and he lifts me sky high. Over his shoulder I can see the group of girls giving me the once over and obviously disapproving of me. I want to shout at them 'I am his sister, you group of dicks' but I refrain and enjoy the attention.

"Wow, Emma you look incredible." Tom eyes me up and down. He always knows how to make a girl feel good.

"You are not so bad yourself big brother. I can see you brought your fan club with you per usual." I point over the girls who act like they have not seen him.

"Not my cup of tea, thanks Em. Way too much make-up and attitude going on for my liking. I really don't have the energy."

"Well at least you get admiring glances, Tom. I would at least like that!" I express as we head out to my car. "I just seem to balls things up." I then proceed to tell Tom about my encounter with James, whilst I was cleaning. He just sits listening and laughing at my expense.

"James would have loved that Em. It is about time you let men see that side of you. You always put an act on when you meet a guy and you are not your true self. You need to let them see you as you are; a funny, live life to the max lovely person. Who is actually as daft as hell."

"Not sure James would agree. I burped on him and sprayed him with polish. Just looks like I am not interested and I am trying to put him off." I share feeling a little subdued as we drive over to our mum's coffee shop.

"Are you interested Em? The reason I ask is because the poor bloke does not need a woman to mess him about. I think the reason he hasn't been with anyone is that he is scared of feeling any hurt. Especially after the death of his dad, which hit him badly." This information makes me really think, as I do not want to hurt him. I am not that kind of person. But it makes me understand him a little more, which is very helpful indeed.

"To be fair Tom, I really don't know James as well as I used to. It is only recently he has started to have chats with me and not just walk on by. I just presumed that the reason he was being polite, was because he was your friend." I add trying to make things clearer in my own mind.

"When we were kids you used to watch him all the time when were playing on our skateboards. James knew you liked him but also knew that you were my baby sister and it was a no-go area. Boys code – I would have hurt him!" Holy moly, this is more news to me.

"Do you think he liked me then?" I ask not sure if I want to know the answer, but this is the first time Tom has shared this kind of stuff with me.

"Yes, I do. He asked about where you were many times. Then shrugged it off like he was glad you weren't there. But I really understood what he was getting at." This reply brings whopping big butterflies to my stomach and I just want to hug myself with pure glee. "You two are just so afraid of rejection and worried about what if it doesn't work? You just need time to get to know each other."

"Blimey Tom, where have these words of wisdom been hiding? I'm really not sure the same brother has come back to stay with me. Who are you and what have you done with my brother? I don't understand why you haven't said anything to me before now?" I ask as we pull up at the coffee shop.

"Listen Emma, we have plenty of time to talk about this, whilst I am here. Let's just say I have learned a lot about myself in London and in my relationship with Lucy." I just nod as I don't want to probe him any further on the matter especially as we are walking up to see our mum. "Oh and one other thing..." Tom whispers. "Boys code was a thing of the past, so anything goes and you can get jiggy with it!" Tom adds as he gyrates his hips in a 'you need to get some of this' manner.

"You really are a plonker." I reply "... and yes with those moves you definitely are my brother. Come on, no more talk about James in front of mum. I am glad you are here so the attention can be deflected from me all onto you." I laugh and link him as we head towards the outdoor seating area.

Mum's beach cafe 'The Cosy Cove' has the most divine view of the bay. She has worked so hard to make her business successful even from before I was born. There are a few local customers sat outside having some morning grub following their early start on the surf. Their boards are all lined up as you enter the seating area and mum has fresh towels for the surfers as they come into the cafe area – a service she says makes her that extra appreciated by her customers. It is a very chilled atmosphere and everyone is chatting amongst themselves, talking about the morning's surf. The furniture is really beach chic; drift wood tables, blue and white painted wooden chairs with blankets and cushions. Mum has even had a couple of hammocks placed around the area, which really are relaxing. I know this from experience, as I fell asleep in one once whilst I was supposedly helping mum out one night. When I woke up I was still in the hammock – didn't even fall out. Very impressive. Heaters are surrounding the outside area for those chilly nights when nobody wants to stay inside. To be honest when you live here, it is all about being outdoors. So, we stay out as much as possible even in those wintry months.

The food at the cafe is just delicious; it's like being at home with mum and dad again. The service board is made out of driftwood and has treats on it such as; hot chocolate with cream and a flake, summer smoothies, soups with hot crusty rolls, bacon and egg sandwiches, ice cold beers and wines. A range of paninis with sweet potato fries and you can even order picnics to take with you onto the beach. At the side of the cafe you can hire paddleboards, surfboards, body boards and kayaks.

This is the side of the business my dad handles and where I spent many days of my childhood helping out or as my dad would see it as 'causing trouble'.

As we walk to the door a number of the local surfers greet me with a nod and a smile and then jump out of their seats when they notice Tom behind me. They shake his hand, say it has been too long and plan to meet up the next morning to surf. Tom is laughing that he will be a bit rusty, but I know that he is an excellent surfer. He would spend many of his mornings riding the waves and even entered a few local competitions performing very well. I had a go a few times, but I would wipe out consistently and then I wouldn't have the energy or willpower to keep trying. I love going out on the paddleboards; now these are very slow and I can control them. The hardest thing is mounting the bugger; you have to get your knees on it and slowly get up on the board or else you are in the water before you know it.

Heading inside we see Mum is putting together some delightful hot pain au chocolate and a latte for a customer. Just makes my mouth water. She glances up and shrieks with pure delight when she sees Tom. She finishes off serving the customer then bounds over to her son with more energy than I have seen in some time.

"Oh Tom, my gorgeous boy. It is so good to see you. You shouldn't wait so long to come and see your old mum." Mum engulfs Tom in a huge cuddle and smothers him in kisses. Mum frowns and holds Tom out to look at him. "You have lost a lot of weight Tom. Are you not looking after yourself? Is it the spilt with Lucy? Oh my poor boy – you are home and mum will feed you up again." The look on Tom's face is priceless. He does not know how to respond to the questioning. I on the other hand just look at him with my smug face, as it is not me in the firing line. "Not to worry now, let's all sit down and have some brunch. I bet you are famished after your long journey here and thank you Emma for picking your brother up. That was very nice of you."

Mum is very cool, down to earth to onlookers. Friends even comment how lucky we are to have such a laid back mum. However, with her children she can be a bit overbearing and controlling. It has driven us round the bend on many occasions with her comments and questions, but we love her dearly and basically tell her when to back off. She knows by this point she has pushed us too far and stops pestering us. This does not happen often, as we usually allow her to do her mum thing and we know it makes her happy. Mum sits us both down on a table made from a surfboard and heads off into the kitchen.

"I see nothing has changed with mum then?" Tom comments before she returns. "Still as full on as usual." He is smiling whilst he is saying this, so I can tell that my big brother is enjoying the fuss.

"Well, you left me to head to London for your dream job. She worries about you and takes it out on me. I just wished you were staying for longer." I add wishfully.

"Let's just say I am thinking of a change of scenery, so a return may be an option." As Tom says this I look up, ready to pounce on him with happiness snuggles when Mum bobs out of the kitchen.

"But, Emma we are not discussing this now in front of mum. The subject is closed." I get the message loud and clear, but inside my little heart is doing ooops up side your head to celebrate. "Here we go, my lovely children. Get your chops around this." Mum places an array of jams, marmalades and honey on the table. Alongside this is a basket of hot pastries and toast. She adds a pot of tea, a filter coffee and a large jug of summer fruits smoothie for us to devour. She really knows me and Tom so well, that we would do anything for her on a full stomach! We sit around chatting and munching on the scrummy food. It is really like the old days and I love the warm feeling it gives me.

"Where is Dad?" Tom asks. "Will he be joining us this morning?"

"He has headed to the fishing port to pick up some fish for me. He will be back later to celebrate your return. I have asked a few friends and family members to join us too. Hope you don't mind. I just need you back here for 7pm – is that okay?" Mum asks, because she thinks she is being polite. But she is not really asking – more telling us that it is okay. We both nod and carry on shoving warm croissants covered with jam and cream into our mouths – one of our personal favourites. We would do anything for our mum right now and she knows it. Clever parenting!

"I am sorry about your split with Lucy. I really did like her." Mum looks at Tom apologetically. She got on with Lucy really well, in fact the best of any of Tom's girlfriends.

"Mum it is fine, honestly. We were both working too much and didn't see each other. She started to get a little closer with one of her colleagues, as she spent that much time with him. She was honest and told me this before it got too messy. As hard as it was I appreciated her honesty and we called it a day." Tom continues to eat, but I can see the hurt on his face, even if he is playing it down. "I think she is with him now, she moved out of my place and in with him. I'm not bitter...much!" I want to cuddle Tom right there. How dare she leave him...my brother..my handsome hero.

"If I ever see Lucy again I shall give her a piece of my mind. Nobody treats my brother like that." I add hoping it will make him feel better. "And anyway it is her loss and our gain." Tom shoots me a quick look as if to say 'keep your trap shut' before I let too much out of the bag. "I'm just saying that it is nice to have my brother home." I say as I place my hand on his arm.

"Well, there are plenty more fish in the sea." Mum adds. "At least you are trying out the fish; your sister on the other hand enjoys her own company far too much. Whilst you are here Tom, try and work your magic for her to find one fish. Even if it is for one night!" Tom and I just look at each other in disbelief at this comment and both start to laugh quite heartily. Wonders never bloody cease with our mother. "You should help me out more in the cafe Emma, there are plenty of men coming and going all day." As she says that a group of young surfers enter for some grub, saying hi to my mum as they pass. I just know she has the urge in her to introduce them to me, but she spies the 'don't you ruddy dare look' on my face. When I returned from my travelling –manless- she had a photo of me under the counter, which she would pop out and show prospective boyfriends. I only found this out when a couple of random guys would walk up to me in the street asking me lots of questions and knowing a great deal of information about me. I finally asked one, how they knew all this stuff and they told me a lady at the Cosy Cove was showing the surfers my picture in the hope of getting a date. As you can imagine I was utterly distraught...humiliated and bleeding angry. She stopped this immediately once the full force of my anger was unleashed on her.

Mum then turns her attention back to Tom. "I thought at your age you would be married by now at the very least. You are supposed to be a role-model for your not so little anymore sister."

"Hey mum, I am doing just fine and I do look up to Tom. How he has handled all this has been so sensible and role-model material." I explain trying to stop her from making Tom feel worse than he already does.

"Listen mother." Tom says very affirmatively. "Things change. I'm glad we didn't get married or we'd be in a messy divorce right now. As for Emma, she does not need me to guide her in life. She is a very intelligent and capable young woman. SO just leave us both alone. Let nature take its course and see where it takes us." I'm slowly losing my appetite – which is so not like me. It is nice to see Tom stand up for us both. Normally we would sit there and just take it off our mum. I take a nice big gulp of my brew and peer at the tension over my mug. They are two of the most stubborn people I know. It is like a standoff at the ok corral. "Please can we talk no more whilst I am here about Lucy, it is a part of my life which is done and I want to move on." Tom's request receives a couple of shrugs from myself and my mum. He knows full well that something will pop up in conversation before he leaves for London. But right now Mum lets it be.

"So you want us back here for 7pm? Or do you need us earlier to help you set up?" I ask in an attempt to break the awkward silence which has engulfed us.

"No, just 7pm. Thank you for the offer though, but I have staff on hand to help out. I am closing the cafe early and setting up. Your dad should be back soon, if you want to wait around?" Mum asks quite hopefully. Tom stands up and kisses Mum on the head.

"Thank you for the food. It was delicious as always. We shall see you all later. I want to head back to Emma's and freshen up." Mum can sense that she has got on Tom's nerves and quickly stands up.

"I am sorry Tom, me and my mouth. No more shall be said on the matter. I am so very glad you are here. I have missed you dearly." Mum embraces Tom in a huge cuddle and grabs me in to join the party.

As Tom and I leave the Cosy Cove the sun is beaming and a gentle, fresh breeze has emerged. It is such a beautiful feeling on my face. Tom and I lean against my car looking out over the bay.

"I know Mum means well, but her comments and questioning are tough to take at the moment." Tom shares taking a deep breath. "Let's head back Emma and get ourselves prepped for the evening ahead." I nod in agreement but we remain standing there for a moment longer watching the paddle boarders heading around the edge of the bay. It is a stunning, calming sight to behold.

Chapter
- Seven -

After an afternoon siesta and a nice long bath we are both suitably refreshed and ready for an evening with the family. I am dressed in my go to favourite comfy outfit; my navy jumpsuit and wedges. Tom looks super handsome in his short sleeved Hawaiian shirt and chinos. I don't think anybody else could rock that look and get away with it. We walk arm in arm back towards the Cosy Cove and it is looking utterly amazeballs. There are twinkly lights, lanterns and huge floor candles scattered around the outdoor seating area. The heaters are on a low setting, as it is not too cold just yet. All the tables have been put together in a long line underneath a banner which reads 'Welcome home Tom'. The fire pit in the corner is blazing away with stacks of marshmellows beside it ready for melting and devouring.

Everything looks shimmering. Mum has excelled herself.

As Tom and I walk into the seating area I spy family members having a catch up alongside some of Mum and Dad's neighbours; whom they have known for years. There are some of Tom's university friends talking to James, Bobby and Poppy. Mum did not tell me she was inviting the Dunn family to our gathering. Jen and her hubby Ben are standing at the cocktail table. They know that mum makes lethal concoctions cocktail mixes and they are getting stuck in. I like their thinking and head over to join them. I load my glass up right to the brim as I stand and watch Tom talking to James. My heart jumps right to my mouth at the sight of him and I take a huge gulp of my drink. James catches me looking over at them, so instead of looking away (which I usually do) I just send a smile back and refill me glass pronto. Need something to combat these nerves, which take over every part of my body when I see him. I do wonder if I have the same effect on him? Then I laugh the thought off as ridiculous. This is going to be a crazy night, what with my crazy mother and my emotions – these are a lethal cocktail mix all on their very own. It feels like drinking a Long Island on speed! Now, if you have ever had a real Long Island from New York City, then you know that they blow your kecks right off and you can't walk straight no matter how hard you try – and I did. I am actually feeling a little wild, which I think is the sudden hit of the cocktails. So I ruffle my hair up and push my knockers out a little. Let's see if I can grab the old boy James' attention just a little more.

Mum looks radiant in her linen pants, gold sandals and floral top. She has a really good body from all the years doing her early morning swims in the sea. I tried it once and shit myself at things that touched me from below and just how bloody freezing it was. My nips got that hard I thought they may have turned to stone and crumbled off my body. My mum actually told me that I would never join her again for the swim, as she couldn't handle the whining and girly screams. She was also embarrassed that the lifeguard on duty thought we were in trouble and headed out to save us. To my total embarrassment, it is something they still laugh about today in the local pub.

My dad emerges from the kitchen, looking tanned and handsome. In fact if you look at Tom they are so similar. A lot of the older ladies in the area swoon when he is around and it is pretty uncomfortable to observe. But just like Tom, he does not care and is oblivious to his effect on women. Dad normally spends his time in the hire shop or taking the kayaks out. You can hire his time and he will take groups out around the bay and he also shares his local knowledge and facts about the wildlife. He is a very clever man and I love going on the tours myself and watching him in action. Fortunately, I wasn't with him when he took a hen party out. The sea got a little bit rough and the water lapsed inside the kayaks. This freaked out a number of the girls and they tippled over. Instead of climbing back in they all scattered about swimming frantically in all directions. Dad called for help and the local RNL came and retrieved the pink ladies from the sea. To this day dad has vowed never to take a hen or stag party out. He was really stressed that night, but all we could do is laugh at the funny side of it all. One of them even handed my dad their number at the end of the day with a message 'captain you can save me any day of the week, call me'. Mum found it hilarious and very attractive.

We are a pretty close family. Tom and Dad are like best friends and it is lovely to observe their bond. This was the total opposite when Tom was in his twenties- they were always at logger heads and Tom would do the opposite of what dad asked. Sounds like me and mum now. Dad gives Tom a big bear hug, which by the way is the best hug in the world. Even Tom enjoys them. Dad makes you feel that everything is alright in the world and he will protect you. An amazing feeling, whatever your mood.

It is time to be seated and our names are written on small blackboard surf boards. Oh how bloody funny, Mum has seated me next to James and Tom is next to Poppy – seems like mum is up to her little match making tricks again. I decide this evening calls for a little more juice, so I head back to the cocktail table and find myself a litre beer glass and fill it. Jen spies me and mimics me puking again. I don't care. As the Mancs say 'let's have it'. I take it back to my table and Dad spots the glass. He knows too well not to comment on my alcohol intake in public, but I know he will have a quiet word with me later. Tom catches my eye and gives me a playful wink and I know he will have Poppy eating out of the palm of his hand in no time. How do I approach James? Recently I have fallen asleep on him, dribbled whilst sleeping and attacked him with polish. I take my seat carefully next to him and smile.

"Evening Emma." He looks cautiously around me avoiding eye contact. "I am just checking you are not armed before I look at you." James says jokingly covering his eyes.

"Not today James." I reply glad that he is making me smile.

"So how is my favourite pop diva doing?" He asks looking straight into my eyes. All I can think of is strip me right now, put your face between my breasts and ravish me. Not sure my family would appreciate it, but I surely would.

"I'm just waiting for my big break. I know it is my time." I add as he laughs at my response. "I've had no injuries busting out my moves thank goodness and you will be pleased to know that there have been zero incidents since that last polish rage attack." The smile he gives me brings me confidence. He actually likes what I say and hasn't taken the piss out of me dancing with the polish.

Mum brings out an array of salads, grilled halluomi, and different types of kebabs on sticks, rice, cheeses and local fish. You can hear the pure delight from everyone in appreciation of what Mum has prepared and they get stuck in straight away.

"Are you as good at cooking as your mum?" James asks placing a huge stuffed pepper in his mouth and making groans, which should be left for the bedroom. I just actually sit and watch him enjoying the pleasure that food gives to him. But thinking my finger could replace the pepper that is currently lapping around his lips.

"Emma?" James jolts me out of yet another fantasy.

"Maybe you could come over one night and judge for yourself?" Well hello Miss Confidence, where have you been hiding? James stops eating and looks at me with a real twinkle in his gorgeous eyes, obviously surprised by my response. As we look at each other neither of us looks away. I feel my hair might resemble Einstein's soon with the amount of electricity passing between us. Before he can reply my dad interrupts the table talk with a small welcome home speech to Tom.

"It's such a joy to see our son, who has been working hard on his journalistic career in London. We have all missed you very much and want you to come home more often. The older your mum and I get, the more we cherish our family time together. We need to enjoy more times like this, as we seem to just meet up for funerals now. Which is all very sad and depressing. As well as welcoming Tom back, we wanted to see everyone and make a pact to keep doing this. Thank you to my wonderful wife Grace for feeding us and organising this. I want you all to now eat, drink and be merry. Can everyone raise their glasses to family and good times." What a great speech from the old man. He never enjoys being centre of attention, but he really hit the nail on the head, it's all about family and happy times to appreciate.

"Sounds like a wedding speech to me." Tom whispers to me. "They are not getting any closer to the altar with either of us, so they are celebrating whatever else they can." We both sit back and laugh, but I feel very proud to be part of such a caring and thoughtful family.

Everyone then continues to dig into the scrumptious nosh.

Wine is flowing nicely and everyone is in great spirits. Tom is chatting and laughing with Poppy. I do get the feeling that she is into him more that he is into her. She keeps touching his arm and ruffling her hair. Lucy who? I can hear echoing in the distance. Poppy is so natural at flirting. I have none of those moves in me and if I start to ruffle my hair I would look like I have been dragged through a hedge backwards! James interrupts Tom and Poppy's flirting to ask if my brother wants to join him for a trip out on his boat one day before he heads back.

"Can I come?" Poppy asks whilst giving her best pout at James. This girl is good and can get what she ruddy well likes out of anyone! Especially with a pout like that.

"Sure only if we can cover you at the cafe...and if you fancy it Emma there is plenty of room?"

Poppy nods eagerly and rubs my brother's arm again. He seems to be enjoying the attention the randy bugger. James looks at me with those delicious eyes. Hmmm just yummy. Who am I to refuse this hunk of burnin' love?

"Yes, I would love to. Only if I can make us a picnic?" I reply.

"Well, if you are as good as your mum at cooking then I bloody can't wait Emma. That would be a great idea." James adds very enthusiastically and seemingly surprised that I said yes. "We will find a nice spot on a secluded beach somewhere and spend the day heading around the bay."

"We are at Jen's tomorrow, so how about Tuesday?" I suggest. Everyone nods in agreement. "It's a date then." James gives me a beaming smile, which would wet anybody's kecks. "I mean it's a plan then." Rephrasing it encase I seem a bit too eager for it to be a date. I can't look too desperate, even if I actually am.

With a mighty stuffed belly and a fuzzy alcohol induced head, I am feeling a little bit hot under the collar so I head over to a hammock. I just need a minute to myself, before I get too carried away with things. I used to worry about getting into hammocks. I was always worried about it flipping right over and that I would look like a dick. I would practise some nights, late on when Mum was clearing up and nobody was around to witness my arse in the air. It paid off, because now I can just swing my body swiftly and I am in. It is so relaxing, swinging here listening to the Cafe Mambo Ibiza music my mum has playing in the background. I just lie there searching out my constellations and of course taking big deep breaths, because in the words of Paul Weller, James does something to me-something deep inside! Oh mama these are emotions I have not had for such a long time. I have loved this man from afar for years and now we are...well I don't know what we are but I sure do like it.

"Something has put a smile on my girl's face." My mum has bobbed over to see me and probably tell me off for being in the hammock. She nudges the hammock. "Come on Emma stop hiding in there and join your friends and family." Holy shit she knocks it some more and I begin to wobble.

"Mum, stop. I will fall out." I hiss trying not to attract the attention of anyone else. But she does not listen and does it again. "Come on Emma, get out and mingle." As she says this my balance is sent right off and the hammock begins to throw me off. I have to put both legs down on either side of it to stop me going arse over tit. Tom spots this and laughs.

"Bloody good job you are wearing pants Emma, or we would be looking at tomorrow's washing." As Tom says this my eyes immediately dart to James' who is blatantly just staring at my lady bits.

"A bit of decorum daughter please." Adds Mum as she swans off; mumbling something about me never going to get a man. I don't even argue back. I feel well and truly pissed off.

After a few more pleasantries with the family, Tom phones us a taxi. We share a ride home with the Dunn crew and lucky me, I get to sit right next to James. In fact, I am nearly on his lap. I am exhausted and decide to put my head on his shoulder. He doesn't shove me off, so I guess he is okay with it. The taxi takes the corner quite sharply, so I cling onto James' arm.

"My James what big muscles you have." I whisper cheekily. These arms are definitely on my man wish list. James just looks down at me and smiles. "My James what shiny teeth you have." I was hoping his response would be 'all the better to eat you with Emma'. Instead he puts his fingers gently to my lips and says "think you have had one too many drinks." I just will him on to be naughty. There must be a naughty side in there. Why is he so scared to show me? I continue to hold his arm and I think I started to sniff him at one point. Just edible! As we arrive at my home, Tom helps me out of the car. We say our goodnights and head inside gently humming 'show me the way to go home'. One of our drunken songs to walk home to – not done this for such a long time. This is a cosy, nostalgic feeling and I want to remember these moments. I just love having Tom home.

Chapter
- Eight -

Pump up those 80s tunes and get out your luminous shell suit for this chapter. Yes I know you have one. We all do...don't we?

Knocking on Jen's front door we can hear the music coming from the back garden. Jen's handsome other half, Ben answers the door and greets us warmly.

"Hello you two. Good to see you again so soon. Jen is with Ava in the back garden Emma, if you want to see her before we put her down for the evening. Tom there is plenty of beer in the kitchen, just go and help yourself mate."

"Think I am in need of a hair of the dog tonight Ben. Felt bloody rough today." Tom adds rubbing his forehead.

"That is because you are now a southerner and can't handle the sweet amber nectar like you used to with us northern blokes. Got a lot of catching up to do mate." Ben and Tom joke as they head into the kitchen. Tom has never been a big drinker anyway, but I think the problem is living here. We always seem to be drinking something, which means we get kind of immune to it most of the time. This coming from the girl who falls asleep drunk and dribbling on the beach. Yep, maybe not so immune on my part.

I walk into the back garden and it looks very pretty. It has a Mediterranean feel to it, with the surrounding garden wall painted white with terracotta pots attached. Begonias and azaleas are in full bloom, with jasmine and clementis trailing around a trellis. The fragrance of lavender hits your nose as pots are scattered around the garden attracting the local butterflies. It is like something from the set of Mamma Mia. I feel like jumping out from one of the pots singing an Abba tune wearing my dungarees. Or an even better thought would be if Colin Firth popped in with his drop dead gorgeous wet my panties smile carrying shots of ouzo. Now that would be perfect. My gorgeous god daughter Ava is dancing away with her mother on the patio. She obviously has good taste in music at such a young age. Must have been the nine months she spent listening to the eclectic range at my home, whilst she was in Jen's womb. I scan around, but there is no sign of James – he must have struggled to get it off work. I feel a bit disappointed and this makes me realise how much I wanted to see him. I shrug this feeling off and give myself a talking to for feeling something. Don't get attached Emma! I have not had this feeling for some time, so I try to shake it off as it is an uncomfortable feeling. Not sure if it should scare me or whether I should embrace it? I take a seat next to Jen and Ava jumps right on me.

"Come here gorgeous girl; give your Aunt Emma lots of kisses!" I cover her with kisses and she does the most adorable giggles. They are so precious to hear. It makes me want to do it some more. "How is my Ava doing today? Did we have Mummy up at a daft time again?" Jen nods at this whilst having a good long sip of her wine.

"Yes she did and decided she wanted to jump on Daddy as well." Ben joins us and hands some chopped up banana to Ava.

"Now remember munchkin. Daddy sleeps, Mummy gets up. I am still training her with this." As Ben says this Jen gives him a sharp dig to his shoulder.

"Cheeky Daddy" says Jen. "He must remember that Ava takes after her mummy and she knows about equality in our household already. So don't listen to him my little cheeky chops." Ava is not listening to either parent; she has crushed up the banana and made a fistful. She then starts to launch it at us. We all stand up immediately apart from Jen – who is obviously used to the food fight and throws some back at her. Ava catches it and shoves it in her mouth. Jen notions to my hair and I can see a large lump of smashed banana dangling on the end.

"Oh, nice Ava. Thanks for sharing." I add.

"Don't worry Emma, I have found out that banana is very good for your hair. Conditions it quite well." Jen raises her glass to me and fishes out more lumps of banana. "Cheers" says Jen and continues to drink her wine.

"Waste not, want not and all that shite..." she adds happily. I just shake my head in pure disgust. I am not cut out for parenting, totally gross.

Ben hands me a new beer to try. He loves his beer and always loves to share any new discoveries. "Here, Emma, try this new grapefruit one." He also likes that I enjoy my beer, as Jen is a wine and gin kind of girl.

"Oh, yes very refreshing." I nod in appreciation. "Can this be like my five a day? Something I could easily have in the morning before work." I lean back on my chair and enjoy the moment. Billy Idol's Wild One starts to play and as if in sync myself and Jen shout 'Pretty Woman'. One of my favourite films. It reminds me of the school holidays and if it was raining or if I felt a little rubbish myself and my mum would put it on and eat trashy food. It was my feel good movie. I know it isn't real, but I still want to go to Rodeo Drive and give them a piece of my mind on how they treated her. Bloody stuck up tossers and something that really bugs me when I watch it. I hate the fact that there are people just like that out there in real life.

"Hi Emma, good to see you again." I turn to see it is Amy again. "Nice of Jen to invite me, when we caught up at the bbq."

"Hi Amy, last time I saw you, you were heading off into a distant dune. Think Jen rescued you."

"Now that is normal for me. I am so used to those dunes that I have been known to sleep in them over night. I always find my way home in the morning."

"Amy that is crazy. Anything could happen to you." I add to the surprised looks on everyone's faces who heard that. You can tell by the look on Amy's face that she really isn't bothered and she will continue to sleep there and not give a stuff about anyone. I like that in her personality, but it is the total opposite of me. I'd think about all the bad stuff that could happen. Probably scare myself shitless with my own imagination more than what could actually happen. That is why I do not and will not watch horror movies. My mind cannot take it and living on my own I would never get a wink of sleep again.

"I have come with a date. He's just at the toilet, but I'm feeling a little nervous, because he is sooo yummy." Amy gives herself a little hug at this thought. "Emma, keep an eye on what I drink, as I don't want to look a knob."

"And you don't want to end up in the dunes again..." I whisper cheekily.

"Now there is a thought. I've heard that he is well endowed, so yes hopefully a rumble in the dunes could be on the cards." As Amy says this we all begin to laugh, but in a uncomfortable manner. Her mystery man is certainly intriguing and you can see everyone's eyes darting to the back door to get a glimpse of Mr Big! Who I am sure is not as good looking as the real one from Sex in the City. "Here he is." Amy points to a man walking across the lawn carrying a set of drinks, with a massive smile on his face. Talking about his face he looks very familiar, but I can't get a clear enough look without making myself too obvious. As he joins us Amy gives him a nervous take me to bed smile. "Everyone, this is Joe. But I'm sure most of you remember him." I peer over my Ray Bans for a better look He is familiar. Oh my word – I can't believe it is him. It's only bloody Joe from high school and he is standing right in front of me. And yes ladies his lips are still like the rim of a blow up paddling pool. However, somehow as his body has grown..in many ways and he has got bigger (get your head from the gutter). Ooh my what a body he has. It is definitely a 'I work out everyday' kind of body. The lips now seem to work and are in proportion to the rest of his body. Thinking back, I recall that I nearly got to taste those lips in high school. He has already had a grope of my bad boys. I push them out in the hope that he sees that I am all woman now, but then swiftly reign my puppies back in realising that shit Emma he is on a date. I'm not that kind of girl, a fella needs to be free or he's not for me! That is my moto and I'm sticking to it. Anyway, after what happened to Tom with Lucy I think my brother would disown me.

"Think I recognise Amy's date over there. Did you date him Emma?" Tom asks sitting beside me.

"Sort of. We were in high school at the time and I nicknamed him rubber lips because they were so big. Mick Jagger would have been envious. But now..." I peer at Joe over the top of my sunglasses to have another look at him.

"Seriously Emma, I can tell he is a player. Stay clear or you will get hurt." Tom looks annoyed at me.

"I'm only looking Tom." I protest. "Anyway he's with Amy. I wouldn't mess with that. She looks happy and mesmerised by him."

"Poor girl. I can see what's coming from a mile away. She is totally oblivious to anyone else here." Tom adds bitterly. I can really tell Tom does not like Joe and he hasn't even spoken to him. I've not seen this side of him before towards another guy. It must be related to his experience with Lucy, so I shut up and don't antagonise the situation. Jen joins us as the Sister Sledge tune Frankie blares out.

"Oh Emma, this is our song. Come on." She pulls me out of my seat and onto the decking. Before I can protest and tell her to piss right off, I am in full flow of our Frankie dance. Standing back to back (which is the obligatory opener); we remember the moves like it was just yesterday. Even Jen's guests are doing their own backing vocals of 'oooohhhs' for us. I spy Joe watching and instead of this making me feel uncomfortable I can see he is singing along and just enjoying the show, so I just embrace it. We finish on the final 'Frankie' and bump our bums together in fits of giggles and sweat.

"We'll get some Bananarama on next. Really show everyone our Nathan Jones groove." Jen mimics the chorus whilst wiping the sweat dripping from her forehead. I grimace as I remember the dance, which we used to perform for Jen's parents in their living room on a daily basis.

"We really made up loads of dances didn't we? Crazy how we remember them."

"I'm knackered after one. How did we keep going when we were kids?" Jen asks catching her breath.

"We were high on Curly Wurlies, Wham bars and Sherbet dips. Remember, we'd eat them when we walked to and from school, for breakfast even. Children today get called for having a bag of crisps for brekkie. It was the norm for us." We both lie back on the grass reminiscing. I love our friendship we have been through so much together and she is part of my family just as much as Tom is.

"Can I join you ladies?" We both look up to see that rubber lips has joined us. I look around to search for Amy, but she is nowhere to be seen.

"You and Emma can catch up. I've got some nibbles to warm up." Jen stands up and leaves us to it the little minx. She knows I'm a mess talking to men, her nibbles could have bloody waited!

"It's good to see you Emma. It's been a long time."

"Yeah, scary how time flies. You look well Joe – not changed much from high school, only bigger." As I say this I know I should have engaged brain first as there are so many connotations linked to this comment. I quickly refocus us. "Where is Amy?" I ask looking around again feeling like I'm doing wrong by talking to him.

"She has just headed back home to let her dog out. She will be back soon. Gives us a chance to catch up." As he says this he nudges closer to me, sending my breathing up a notch. "I noticed you're not married yet." He notions to my wedding finger. "Anyone else in your life at the moment?" As he says this I want to say James, but know that it is just some harmless flirting and nothing more. I'm sure he would have been here tonight if he wanted to see me. This thought pierces my heart a tiny bit.

"No, nobody in particular." I change the subject quickly. "Done any head bumping with anyone lately?" I ask with a smirk. He begins to laugh as he understands the reference to the incident in the playground. "Can I ask, what did you tell everyone about what happened with us?" I'm not afraid to ask all these years later, curious more than anything.

"Not really sure now. I do remember it because I started going out with Ana. Sorry if it upset you in anyway. I was a bit of a jerk back then." I'm surprised by his apology but not really sure if he is sincere. I just can't suss him out. Maybe Tom has this guy all wrong? I give his handsome face a once over. His jaw line is so masculine and strong, very David Gandy like. He has big brown puppy dog eyes, which have probably done a lot of begging and apologising in their time. His dark hair is much shorter than I remember and it seems like he has a tub of gel on it. Couldn't ruffle any fingers in there. Then there's the lips...still as big as ever but very juicy looking if I may say so. He catches me looking at his lips and he smirks to himself. Shitting Nora Emma, he knows he is good looking and loves that I am checking him out. I give myself a good telling off...again. Don't give him any ammo and definitely don't show him that I like him. Like him? Have I just said that? Oh boy roll over Beethoven here is another guy who is totally bad for you and yes you guessed it – it makes my insides go to mush. He has a mischievously naughty side to him and I like that. It has always been something that suckers me into a man. In the words of Bobby Brown 'My mind is telling me NO, but my body's telling me yes.'

"I think I told them I got to a base with you. Not sure which one now, but I remember the boys being impressed."

"Impressed? How?" I asked curious at this comment.

"Well, nobody could break through your ice wall. Every day we saw this hot little, blonde surfer chick coming into school and she didn't really show interest in anyone." Wow, this really is news to me.

"Are you kidding? Nobody was really interested in me. I didn't go out late and hang out in the park with everyone. I just stayed at home and did my studies. I was not made of ice."

"Then you really have no idea, because at the park you were a topic of conversation on many nights. I seemed to have got the furthest with you." Joe laughs at this comment and adds.. "and that was only because we bumped heads and I got a cheeky grope in."

"I was actually in love with Matthew Hill, but all he wanted was to be in the friend zone." Probably still am in love with the idea of being with him now. I used to have dreams that he was Danny Zuko and I was Sandra Dee and we'd be eating burgers at the drive in together.

"Funny that. I definitely recall Matthew saying that the best way to get a snog from you would be by becoming mates first." Now this comment makes me sit the hell right up. It was a planned friendship?

"What the bleeding hell?" I think I'm actually going to combust.

"Yeah, he said he would play hockey or something against you and you'd jump on each other when you scored. He seemed to like this a great deal." Oh lordy, lordy. He is telling me this now? Why did I not have a clue about this? I feel like heading on a plane to New Zealand and giving him a piece of my bloody mind. The dick would probably not remember me now though.

"Crikey Joe, this is a lot to take in. Why share this with me now?" But I don't really listen to his answer I see out of the corner of my eye that James has arrived and is looking around. We catch each other's eye and as I wave he sees that I am talking to Joe, so he swiftly turns and walks away. Didn't even acknowledge me. Was he mad? After this whole load of new information I really do not have a clue about men. I need to stop trying to figure them out. It is simple they want sugar as much as possible and they find the sweetest one to nibble, no questions asked. Does that mean I was sugar to Matthew? Not sure how to take this, so I decide I need a break from discussing this and begin to stand up. Right at the perfect time that Amy walks back through the doors and slumps down on Joe's lap. I head quickly into the kitchen to help Jen dish up some food. Best thing for me to do now is eat. Always makes me feel better.

I start chopping a bunch of carrots up and place them on a dish with some hummus.
"What have the poor carrots done to you?" James asks as he enters the kitchen. I give him one of my Cheshire Cheese smiles and continue to chop.
"Oh nothing. Glad to see you could get time off work James."
"Really? I'm surprised you noticed." His reply is sharp and blooming nasty. Jen raises her eyebrow at me. I decide not to rise to it, which is very unlike me.

"I noticed the minute you walked into the garden as a matter of fact. Now make yourself useful and take these into the garden." I shove bowls of grub into his hands and he heads out.

Jen scurries over to me "He's pissed you were talking to big lips. I saw his face Emma, he is seriously jealous."

"Well he had better be a man and toughen the hell up if he wants anything to do with me. I am a WOMAN and I need a real man. No farting about allowed. I had to put up with that shit in high school."

"Hell yes, cheers to that Emma!" we clash our drinks together in a very manly way.

"Anything else you'd like me to serve ladies?" James has arrived back to help.

"You on my bed." I mutter under my breath and begin to giggle.

"Sorry?" James asks.

Oh shit I have to think quick, but I freeze. Jen to the rescue.

"I have an apron you can have James. Go on put it on and give us ladies a treat." Jen winks at him.

"and nothing else." I mutter again.

"I would actually like to have a chat with Emma. Can I steal her away Jen?" I look up at James with total surprise. Maybe he has some balls in there after all.

"Lead the way." I throw my pinnie at Jen and follow behind his sweet tush.

We take a seat on the sofa in the playroom. It's really quiet in here as everyone is out back. He has placed a drink for each of us either side of the sofa, which I think is a nice touch. As we both sit down, we are conscious of touching each other or a little nervous so we leave a small gap between us. James picks up his beer and begins to drink. He really looks nervous – not sure if he is coming up for air?

"James, is everything okay?" I ask in the hope he will stop drinking and look at me. But he just nods and carries on drinking. The silence is killing me. Not sure what he wants to talk about, but there is feck all talking going on. Impatience brewing through my body, I begin to stand up. James grabs hold of my arm.

"Please stay, I have something I need to say. It's just taking me a minute to say it." I sit back down and turn myself to face him.

"I'm here James, say whatever it is. I'm a good listener. Totally understand if you are not into me. I'm used to it James to be honest." I say matter of factly, because I am. I'm fed up of men pretending that I am what they have been looking for. I just want honesty and someone to really want me no messing about.

"Emma, that's not what I was going to say." He seems to have his courage back and he faces me.

"I need to get this off my chest before whatever this is that is going on between us goes any further." I don't interrupt – which is yes very unusual for me. He has my full undivided attention. "You must be aware that when I lost my dad, my whole world fell apart. Everything was an utter daze. Wasn't sure if I was coming or going for such a long time." James is so handsome and watching him unsure of himself playing with his fingers, it is a sight to behold. "I had to be there for my mum and Poppy. Bobby didn't talk to me about it, as it's not what blokes do. We just get on with it. But inside it tore me apart. The only way I got myself through the pain was to work on the Boat Yard. It made me feel closer to my dad and the long days made me stop thinking about the heartache. It also brought an income into our home, which Dad had provided." He takes another long sip of beer and a deep breath. I say nothing. "I closed myself off to everyone. If I felt I was getting close to someone I would call it a day. All because I was afraid of feeling anymore pain. I just couldn't handle it."

"I understand James, but that's one thing people cannot promise as they do not know the future. You may need to just put yourself out there and have a little hope and belief that life can be good."

"Yeah, I agree that's why I am talking to you now. I am putting myself out there. I should have done it many years ago with you."

"Oh?" I asked surprised.

"I've always loved your fresh, beautiful face from being your neighbour. Your smile would make everything better in an instant. The butterflies I get when you are around is something my body can't fathom. When we were kids I didn't go there due to the bro code. Then when I got older my dad died and I shut myself off from life." What is happening tonight? I've just had rubber lips tell me I was seen as something of a treat at high school, now the man whom I have lusted after for nearly thirty bleeding years is telling me he has had similar feelings. Am I still knocked out lying by the side of my toilet seat dreaming this shit up? Or is it actually happening? As James faces the window I start to pinch my arms, then my thighs. No I'm wide awake and that sodding well hurt! It is really refreshing that he is telling me this, but I'm not sure I believe it. Is this the cleverest trick in the man book? Tell a girl you have always liked her and score you're on the home run. Words are not coming out. My mouth has dried up. I'm confused and unsure how to respond to his honesty. Just then rubber lips Joe comes bounding in the room and pulls me right out of my seat.

"Come on Emma. I've got our common room song on Michelle Gayle's Sweetness. Remember dancing to this on the pool table?" I just nod as he pulls me away from James and into the back garden and everyone is on their feet. James follows and looks very confounded. In fact, everyone looks well oiled and on their merry way. Joe begins to bump his hips into mine.

I spy James leaning against the door talking to Tom. I get myself fully engrossed in the song as I truly do love it. Not sure where Amy has gone? But Joe is the life and soul of the party. He is shimmying up to Jen and twirling her under his arms. Most of the ladies have left their male partners and are now surrounding Joe busting out his moves on the grass.

I decide to call it a night and try to finish my talk with James. I look back over to where James was stood, but he has gone. As I head towards the exit the cheeky chappy Joe grabs my hand and whizzes me into his arms. Oh my, so strong and commanding. His tight grasp makes me dizzy. I can feel his muscles rippling onto my chest and it makes all my hairs stand to attention. Yes sir! This guy really knows how to have fun and make everyone around him feel at ease.

"We must meet up soon Emma. I've got your number off Jen. I will give you a call." Joe kisses my hand as Tom interrupts and cuts in.

"Come on sis, we need to be heading back. Got a boat trip tomorrow." I say my goodbyes and leave watching Joe standing on a chair doing his own Full Monty routine. I try to stay but Tom keeps pulling me further away. I sulk all the way home.

"Do you really want to get involved with a guy like that Emma? Don't make the mistake I did and be fooled by their over-confidence. As attractive as it may be, it comes with whole load of other shit. And he has trouble written right through him like a piece of Blackpool rock."

Tom can say what he likes, I'm really not listening. All I can think about is that I missed a Magic Mike moment and I don't often get many of them in my life around here!

Chapter
– Nine –

Okay me hearties, strap yourself in because it's gonna be a bumpy ride!

We arrive early doors at the boat yard, ready to meet Poppy and James. I have spent the night having very nice dreams about very hot men doing dancing around me; including rubber lips and James. Not got much sleep, but it was bloody worth it. As we board his boat, James presents us all with a bacon butty and a flask of tea to start the day and it is truly welcomed.

"If we were married James, would you have a bacon bap ready for me every day?" I ask. Think I'm still pissed from the night before, as I don't know how that crept out of my mouth.

"Bacon, eggs, sausages..whatever takes your fancy." He responds with a mischievous twinkle in his gorgeous eyes. I take a huge bite out of my bap. Delicious.

"Take me down the aisle now. But you must be warned, I will grow truly fat. As I rarely do any exercise."

"I think we could arrange some sort of exercise for you Emma." Now, is he thinking what I am thinking about the type of acrobatic exercise, swinging from the bleeding chandeliers type exercise? Hope so.

As we sit there on the boat, I'm watching James get everything prepared for our day. He really knows his stuff and it is a very attractive quality in a man. He pops over with a life jacket for me to put on. I place it over my head and allow him to strap me in. He pulls it ever so tightly and it catches my breath. Is it too early for a wine? Need some help making it through today or I may just pounce right now on the poor man.

"Hope it's not too choppy today." I say praying to the gods. I really like the idea of going out on a boat, but if it starts to bump and grind about I will see my bacon butty again very soon.

James takes to the wheel and steers us away from land. Tom and Poppy look very cosy indeed – think this sight alone may make me want to vomit. He does look happy though and that is all I want, but oh help me if she hurts him. Baby sister will take on the role of protector and go a little ape shit on her. Think I better give her the heads up about Tom's previous relationship and she had better treat him well. I decide to join James up front, but I become unbalanced with the jerking motion of the boat. It sends me toppling forward head butting James in the rear...totally undignified.

"Bit early to be going there Emma?" James shouts laughing at my tricky legs. I grab hold of the side of the boat and steady myself, trying to laugh along at my ridiculousness.

"Where did you get to last night? We didn't finish our conversation." I ask.

"Well knob head, or whatever he is called took you away, so didn't really get chance to finish it." Crickey, never really heard James swear. I like it.

"Well, as for your thoughts, thank you for telling me. I often wondered why I hadn't seen you with women. I see the women lining up that's for sure." This makes him smile and it eases the bit of tension between us.

"Did you go home with that guy from high school?"

"No, James I am not like that at all. He is fun, but he was with Amy and he's not into me that way."

"Don't be so sure Emma, I saw the way he looked at you." I quickly change the subject as yes I did see the way he looked at me and it knocked my woolie bed socks right off.

"So, you said that you have liked me since we were kids?" Let's go in for the kill! He stops steering and looks directly at me. "Then stop messing James and stop thinking about things too much."

"Do you want to steer Emma?" He asks. As I am about to say yes, Poppy bounds over and takes the wheel from James.

"Come on Tom." She shouts. "I want to show you how it's done." She pushes her brother off the wheel and begins to teach Tom. There is a lot of touchy feelie going on and I feel the band from the bloody Titanic may start up soon. BRRR I really don't want to be watching this.

"Here Emma, take a look in my cool bag and get yourself a drink." As James hands over the bag, our hands brush together and in the words of Danny Zuko 'it's electrifying'. As I open the box, feeling a little shaky there are cans of cold beer and bottles of prosecco nestled in the cold ice. Now we are talking, this should calm my nerves. I pull out a bottle of fizz and proceed to pop it's cork. It is a real cracker and flies high up into the air. I don't even ask for a glass. I give the rim a wipe and start to drink from the bottle. My mother would cry in despair if she knew I was doing this. Makes it all the more sweeter. The prosecco is so fizzy that the first gulp goes straight to my nose, making my eyes water. James is oblivious to this thank goodness and stretches out beside me relaxing.

"Cheers. Here's to good times." He raises his drink to me.

"I will cheers to that." I reply.

"Poppy and Tom seem to be getting on well." James observes.

"Does it bother you?" I ask.

"It used to. I'd threaten anyone who went near my sister. Funny though with Tom I know he is a good guy, so it doesn't bother me much at all."

I stretch out beside James and look out at the incredible view surrounding us. It is breathtaking and relaxes me to the core. However, I realise it really is not as gorgeous as the man that is sat beside me.

"James are you seeing anyone at the moment?" I need to know before I make a fool of myself.

"No, what about you?"

"No, I've made such bad choices with blokes. I'm just terrified to make the same mistakes again."

"Well, they are idiots. You are beautiful Emma and any man would be lucky to have you." He turns to face me as my blush starts at my chest and rises to my forehead.

"Thanks James, that's very nice of you to say. You have always been pretty decent to me, even growing up." He moves closer and I can't stop staring at his lips.

"I was decent because all the other boys were mean to you. What I mean is the other boys fancied you, so they were mean. So, I thought I may stand out from them by doing the opposite."

"Here you go Emma, have a turn on the wheel." Tom shouts as I'm about to delve a little more into his comment. "Come on James, show Em what to do. It's just amazing. I feel free." James takes my hand in his. Oh my. He guides me over to steer. No argument needed, I just follow. I hold on for dear life and he stands behind me. Boy he feels so good and smells intoxicating. He gently holds my hands over the wheel. His hands tick all the boxes on my wish list; big, strong and well trimmed nails. He is all man. I can see his veins bulging and this sends my mind into a tizz. Don't know what possesses me but I start to trace them with my finger. This makes James jump and we both lose our balance.

"We are here," shouts Poppy. She is pointing to what the locals call Cast Away Beach, as everything gets shipped up here. It can only be accessed by boat or abseiling down the rock face. "It looks like we have it all to ourselves as well." She squeals delightedly. I really wished Poppy and Tom weren't with us now. I have the feeling something maybe going down and I hope it's James...on me!

In order to reach the beach we have to wade a little in the water and carry everything. I have to hitch my skirt up right to my bum to stop me getting too wet. We all have a rucksack on and carefully paddle to the beach. The sand here is totally beautiful. It's so gentle and soft on your skin, you get a real exfoliation like at a spa. We roll our picnic blankets out and Tom links his phone up to a small speaker. The gentle tones of Chris Issac's begin to fill the air. I just lie back and enjoy the view of James emerging from the water. If I squint he is naked, wet and smouldering like James Bond. I could be his Pussy Galore. What a thought.

"What's for lunch?" Tom asks.

I sit up and proceed to take out the contents of my ruck sack. "We have a range of cold sandwiches, pittas and feta. Here's some salad with dressing if you like. Some crisps and dips with chopped peppers and carrot sticks. A box of pork pies here and some spicy samosas if you fancy."

"Looks like a feast fit for a king." Announces Poppy chirpily. We all snuggle on the blanket digging into the grub. I seem to have lost my appetite. Every time I look at James another knot arrives in my stomach and I just can't bear the thought of eating. I just end up grazing on an egg sandwich.

"Thanks to James for organising this and to my little sister for the food." Tom hands us all a glass of vino and we all cheers.

After lunch, Tom and Poppy head for a walk paddling their feet in the sea and splashing each other. James drops on his knees next to me with his cooler bag of alcohol. "Champagne Emma?" He asks.

"Oh yes please." I answer a bit too eagerly.

James pulls out some plastic flutes and pops the cork in an expert manner.

"I have been saving this for us Emma. My sister would demolish this if she knew I had it." I open the tub of stuffed olives and jalapenos with cheese and begin to tuck in.

"Really appreciate you coming today Emma."

"It was nice of you to offer and it's actually nice to finally get to know the real you after all these years."

"Cheers to that. I finally feel like I can enjoy life. Losing Dad broke something in me and although I'm not mended, I do feel like I deserve to be happy." James looks out thoughtfully to sea. It is so quiet that I can hear the gentle popping of the champagne bubbles. I gently lean towards James and give him a soft kiss on his cheek. He moves his head and we are looking directly into each other's eyes. Boy I wish I knew what he was thinking. I gulp and I can instantly smell his breath as he moves closer to me. He places his hand behind my head and gently pulls me closer until our mouths meet. His lips are wet and so fine. I feel like I am a teenager again in this moment. My heart is leaping all over the bloody show. I open my eyes to see just how gorgeous this man is before me. He has been nothing but honest and he hasn't messed me about. All I want to do is pounce on him, but I refrain and enjoy this lip smacking snog. James eventually stops and pulls away. I on the other hand stay in the same position with my eyes closed enjoying the throbbing of my lips (both sets in fact).

"Emma, you take my breath away." He whispers.

"James, just do me a favour?" I ask. "Please bring your lips right back here. I've not finished with you yet." The smile on his face entangles my heart and he lunges in before I need to beg. This time it is a little more rough and desperate. Our hands are flying everywhere.

"It's about time." Shouts Poppy over to us. I go beetroot red and feel very self-conscious.

"Come on Emma, let's go and explore." James stands up and holds his hand out for me to take. We walk along the beach just holding the tips of our fingers together. This moment feels very surreal like I am having an out of body experience. This could be one of my movie dreams.

We bob over to explore the small, hidden caves underneath the cliff edge. As you enter the chill hits you and it sends a quiver down your back bone. You can see the water level mark on the side and it is very clear they get flooded when the tide comes in. This unsettles me a little and I hold onto James' hand tightly, dithering a bit pathetically. The water is dripping onto our heads making me giggle. I look up and an almighty droplet hits me eye.

"Bloody Nora." I shriek. James laughs and uses his thumb to dry away the excess water rolling off my face. As he does this a whole load of lust and wanton just engulfs me and I throw myself at him wrapping my legs around his waist. Firstly, my thoughts are of how impressive my jump was - my high school gym teacher would be proud. Secondly, my thoughts turn to worry that he thinks that I'm weird and desperate (which I am guilty of both), but his body is just as happy as mine at the leap of faith. He tugs my hair back, opening my neck line and he goes full on Dracula and sucks away up and down until he reaches my lips again. Now if a guy tugs your hair in the manner he did, you would probably give him a slap. On this occasion he took me totally by surprise and I allowed myself to be open to something new. In this moment I wanted to make my own memorable piece of life, just like in the movies. I twirl my fingers in his mane and nibble on his lips. We mould together so perfectly, I have never been so in sync with a man before. He continues to hold me up clasping his hands on my buttocks and rubbing his thumb firmly over my bum cheek to generate pure arousal all over my derriere! It really is not a pretty sight to be an observer of, but when you are full on into the nitty gritty of fumbling, who gives a rats arse?

As we emerge from the cave, my smug face says it all and if you thought my hair looked bad in the morning, you ain't seen nothing yet. Even Rod Stewart would leg it frightened. We stroll back to the picnic and help Tom and Poppy tidy everything up. I look like the cat that got the cream – my smile is bigger than the Cheshire cat as we head back home. Even the sway of the sea does not dampen my jovial mood.

Chapter

- Ten -

The beast from the east has arrived. It is time to batten down the hatches. I don't know but something about wild weather, changes something in my personality. I end up looking like Sigorney Weaver in Ghostbusters when she is possessed. My hair has a mind of its own and I wear the daftest stuff to reflect my mood (thinking I look good).

The news has told us that we are going to feel the wrath of hurricane Irene and have been warned not to leave our homes unless it's an emergency. It's a bloody good job we didn't head out on the boat today – looking out from my apartment I can see the huge waves pounding the beach below me.
It takes me back to when Tom and I were kids, we used to put our rain macs on and head down to the beach on

days like today. We would stand there and let the waves bash us. We would be absolutely drenched through and we'd love every minute. There would be nobody on beach patrol to tell us off. Nobody was really arsed what we did when I was growing up. It secms like risk assessment hell whatever you do nowadays and kids get told off for everything. There'd be some nights when my mum didn't even know where we were. She just knew our bellies would rumble and we would head home. Totally different to attitudes today, but then society around us has changed and got a lot more seriarse (serious with arse as my dad would say).

I've had a couple of messages today from the hunk of burnin' love James checking on me; he's such a gentlemen. He has headed to the boat yard to secure the premises and ensure all the boats are moored up safely. It does cross my mind (swiftly) to go and check on him, but I just can't seem to move my backside off the comfy sofa. I've heard Tom's phone buzz a number of times this morning with Poppy's name flashing up.

"Are you answering the poor girl dearest brother?" I ask as he looks over at his phone flashing.

"She is great fun and full of life, but a bit full on."

"Then don't string her along, be honest with her."

"I've told her that I am heading back soon, but this doesn't seem to bother her."

"I think it's you who hasn't pushed the matter. I think you are liking the attention and wanting your cake and eating it." Tom laughs at this but knows I am right. "Please don't mention going home. I hate the thought of you leaving and that means I have to return to work. Boooo with cherries on top."

"Ah, but you have the mighty James now to keep you company. Have you planned to meet up soon?"

"Yes, we are supposed to be meeting at the Surf Festival. Are you still coming or do you have other plans?"

"I wish I was competing to be honest, I've missed surfing. I will come, as long as I'm not getting in the way of you love birds."

"Love birds? I like the idea of that, but no you are never in the way. I am going out with the girls tomorrow night and before you ask you are not invited. So you need to find somebody else's company to keep. Maybe Mum and Dad?"

"I may see if James wants to do a pub crawl round the locals...all four of them!"

"Oh? Just for a drink?" Feeling a teeny bit jealous.

"Don't be jealous Em, I will keep my hands to myself."

"I trust you, it's other women I don't trust. He is just too yummy to resist."

"Emma he only has eyes for you, trust me you have no need to worry." I'm not sure where this possessiveness has come from within me but, it's pretty ugly to hear coming out of my mouth.

"It's okay; he's single still we haven't even been on a proper date yet, just the two of us. We may not even like each other." I know in my heart this is not true, because even if we didn't talk, we would have plenty more of 'how's your father' to be getting on with. "Mum says that the reason her marriage to Dad has lasted so long, is because they don't really talk. She says they don't talk, so they don't argue. Sounds like a good relationship to me."

"Yep, good job really because Dad is a man of little words. You have to be a mind reader sometimes around him. It can actually drive you a little bonkers. Must admit though, Lucy used to talk non-stop and look at us now. Maybe there's something in it."

"Do you miss her?" I ask tentatively as the wind begins to hammer my windows.

"I did. Doesn't bother me as much now. Don't know how I'd handle seeing her again though and if she is with him, I think I may punch him in the mush."

"Is she the reason why you are thinking of moving back here?"

"Partly, yes. Partly I've had enough of the pace of my life. Blink and you would have missed the last few years in London. I want that to stop and slow down. I know that by moving back here, I would be putting myself first."

"Doing journalism still?"

"I will see what is out there to offer me. There's no rush." This comment saddens me. I want there to be a rush. I want there to be the perfect job for my brother, so he can head home as soon as possible.

"You can always stay with me rent free until you find your feet."

"Cheers Em that's kind of you to offer. I will have a think, but you may not want me to cramp your style - what with James on the scene."

"Don't get carried away. I'm not." Which is a right old bloody lie, as I went to bed with plans of 'me and James' in my head last night and it's all I have thought about today.

I head onto the balcony to bring in my furniture which is heavy, but it is starting to be knocked about. As I head outside the force of the wind knocks me backwards and takes my breath away a little. I pick up my plant pots and tuck them near the window and as I am doing this the rain starts to pour. It's full on pelting me, like being in a shower. Laughing inside my nice, warm and cosy apartment Tom tries to move his arse to help, but he is finding the whole scene too funny. My wet hair is slapping my face, my feet keep slipping on the decking and my hands are becoming cold and sore. He finally heads out as he sees that I am struggling with the table and it is like an episode from the Chuckle Brothers. It takes us ages to navigate it through my doors. At this point we are drenched.

"Come on Emma, follow me." Tom heads back onto my balcony. "Just look at the power of this storm." We both stand there as the wind and rain pelts us, but it really is mesmerising. Looking onto the horizon, the sky is bewitching and brewing. It has plans for us and it looks like it is ready to put on a lightning show. Nature at its finest. We head inside, pull our chairs up to the window and watch the performance commence. The sheets of lightning highlight the ocean and the thunder bangs right above us. No matter how old we get, we still count to see how far it is away.

"1, 2, 3.." Crack the thunder hits. "Ooooooh, it's close." I run and grab my blanket and some towels and we get ourselves dry and snugly. "Put the kettle on Tom, I'm in need of a brew and some shortbread."

"I'm on it." Tom jumps from the chair and runs into the kitchen to put the kettle on. "Can you pause the show Em, so I don't miss anything. You don't get anything like this in London. I've missed a good old storm." Tom literally skips in with the biscuits in hand.

"I've missed enjoying watching them with you Tom. Reminds me of when we were little. I was just thinking about our wave dodging days when a storm would arrive. You couldn't get us back inside."

"Oh yes, I remember. I loved getting home and mum would have a nice hot bath ready for us and she would have our PJs warming on the radiator. Made us feel so snugly."

"Ah, so nice. Dad would make the best cheese on toast and we would watch Big Foot and the Hendersons." I miss my brother so much and these memories are wonderful, but I want to make new ones with him. He arrives back as the lightning streaks across the ocean knocking out the power to the area. We sit in the dark, laughing. "At least we got a brew before the power went out. Cheers Em." This is lovely jubley!

Chapter
- Eleven -

Tom heads out to meet James for a session on the beer. I warn him to be good and get him to ask some subtle questions to James about what he thinks about me. I warn my brother that it will be twenty questions tomorrow, so he is not allowed to say that he 'doesn't know'.

Now he has left it allows me time to get my booty all prepped for a night out with the girls. I'm kind of excited, as it's not very often we get our diaries to match on a date, so this is a bloody miracle in itself. Nobody (as yet) has ducked out on us. I shimmy on over to my phone and blast my playlist out. Tunes are so important to the 'getting ready' stage of the evening. The first tune that starts up is from the Rocky film 'Hearts on Fire' - I love this song. It makes me want to do some upper cuts and pretend skipping on the spot. It gets my heart going that's for sure. Jabbing and dodging I head into the kitchen and pour myself a nice G&T and add some raspberries. Much healthier than a beer! I will save the beer for later. I know if I start on it now, I won't be able to button up any pants as I will be bloated. Later on I won't give two hoots what I look like.

Heading to the bathroom I start my bath and add plenty of bubble bath to soak in. Not had a going out bath for a long time, so I'm going to make it special. I find some candles, turn the main light switch off and enjoy the seductive ambience it creates. I place my G&T on the side and slip in. It soon makes all my muscles relax and I lie there enjoying my tunes and feeling very girly indeed. Now if you are like me, then you like the idea of a bath, but can't stay in it for too long. After a few minutes I get a little fidgety. I tell myself off and lie back again –closing my eyes trying to make myself enjoy it. I start to over-heat and then worry that I am stewing in my own dirt. Not that I am a dirty bird, it's just the thought of dirt floating around me. Sitting up I take a nice gulp of my drink and play with the bubbles. I start to blow them and they are sticking to the bathroom walls. This is more like it. I try to think of myself as

Kylie Minogue in the 'I should be so lucky' video. I know what you're thinking – yes you should be so bloody lucky! That's it I've had enough, so I give my legs a quick shave and head to the shower to rinse off the bubbles. My face has a lovely glow to it; at least I won't need too much bronzer tonight.

I've noticed that it has stopped raining thank goodness, so I can wear pants or a dress. Looking in my wardrobe I don't really have that many options. Black top, black jeans, black cardigans, black on black. I really must get some colour injected into here. It is so depressing. I vouch to go out shopping with Jen soon and funk my clothing up a little bit. I spy a blue, floaty dress that I haven't worn for some time. I put it on, but notice that it hangs off me in a rather naff and unflattering way. Adding a belt makes it look better and I can ruffle the dress over it, so when I do drink a beer later on nobody will see my beer gut hanging out...perfect! It looks pretty good on, but my pale legs stick out like a sore thumb. I find some wash off fake tan and rub it in. When it gets dark outside nobody will see my legs to be honest, but I want to look good for me and a little fake tan perks up my confidence. So long as it doesn't rain I am good, as it will streak like hell. As I'm blow drying my hair I just can't resist dancing in front of my floor mirror. Nobody is here and my door is locked, so nobody will witness me shaking my thing in my knickers and bra. Hooked on a feeling starts to play. Oooooh thoughts of Chris Pratt asking me to dance cross my mind and I am transported into another world, where we get our freak on. Why can't I dance like this when I am out? Not bragging (much) but I look good. My underwear is even matching, which is a very rare thing. My hair is looking bouncy and I have a bubble bath / G&T glow. Surely, if the Prattmeister saw me like this, he would come and get his love on! However, it could quite possibly be my G&T goggles that are on? Just saying, that life looks a whole lot better through them and so does my wobbly body. That is my plan for if James ever sees me like this; low lighting and lots of beer. I take my time to do my make-up, as I don't want eye liner over my forehead. I take it ever so steady to try and not to look like a clown. I spritz my whole body, even my lady parts with some perfume and take a look at myself.

My phone starts to buzz, it is Jen outside waiting in the taxi. I grab my handbag and excitedly head out.

We head into The Shack Bar where we meet with the rest of our group. These girls are locals whom we went to college with and have stayed friends. They are great fun and like the freedom of being out. It's the married ones you have to watch as the freedom can send them a little crazy. They've normally passed out by 11pm, as they have necked their drinks through pure giddiness about being out without their partners. I on the other hand take it steady Eddie and I can go all night long. My main love is to dance, some nights I am not even bothered about drinking, I would just strut my stuff on the dance floor or around the chairs. I don't even care usually who is watching me – I've normally finished man hunting by this stage and just enjoy myself. Tonight is a little different, I'm not on the hunt and it feels very relaxing. Jugs of cocktails are covering the tables and the girls are already in full swing. They cheer when they see us and we all give each other big hugs and kisses. It is such a nice feeling, that no matter how long ago we met up it is just like yesterday and our friendship is just as strong. The bar is full and rocking tonight. The DJ has some 90s dance hits pumping out and there is a real good vibe amongst the crowd, who are jigging along. The girls have pushed their chairs back and are starting to dance around the table. Ultra Nate's Free comes on and you can hear the girls in unison shout "TUUNNEE". Our group seems to be attracting a lot of male attention tonight. Men keep bobbing over to chat and try to join in with the dancing, but nobody is interested. Girl power and all that shite! Let's hear it for the girls.

Jen heads to the bar and whenever she does it always worries me, as she can bring back the worst concoctions ever. I remember playing a game of cards with her and she said the loser downs a drink. Do you know what drink she bought? A Bloody Mary. Yes that's right – it makes me want to be sick right now thinking about the shitty drink. Do you know who kept losing? Correct again, yes me. Worst game of cards I have ever played.

"Come on Emma let's do some cement mixers." She shouts with a twinkle in her eye. "It will remind us of being back at college." My face says it all. I would rather have a Bloody Mary right now. Ever had a cement mixer before? NO? Good, lucky you. You jammy sod.

"Why Jen? Why do you make us drink crap all the time?"

"Right, moaner. Shut up and put the Baileys in your mouth." I do as I am told, but for the record – I am not happy.

"Now add the lime...and shake it." I have to shake my mouth like a washing machine, so the drink congeals in my mouth. I start to gag and Jen shakes her finger at me as if to say 'don't you bleeding dare spit it out'. "Now swallow." She commands. Shitting Nora, it is like I have been sick and re- swallowed it. "Wipe you face Em, you have congealed dribbles."

"Jen, that is just as fecking, bollocky naff as ever. Now it's your turn." Not one moan comes out of her mouth, she grabs the drinks and mixes them for some time. She looks like she is rinsing her mouth with mouth wash, not drinking a cup of sick.

"Daddaaa." She sings triumphantly.

"Nothing to be proud of my love." I add in a grump. I grab a bottle of beer from the table and down it. Don't know who it belongs to and at this moment I don't care. That is until someone taps me on the shoulder.

"I think you'll find that was my beer you demolished in one gulp." I turn and look into the eyes of a fine young man. Looks a little younger than me, but he looks like he has just stepped off the Strictly Come Dancing programme. "Don't think I've seen a woman as petite as you drink a beer that fast. Most impressive."

"Oh, I'm truly sorry. My so called friend made me do a crappy shot and I needed relief pretty fast. I will get you a new one." I reply very shyly and head to the bar quickly before he says anything else to me.

"Here you go and sorry again." I hand him his beer and go to turn away.

"I'm Luke; you didn't need to buy me another. In fact I was going to ask you if you wanted one before you nicked my beer."

"Hi, I'm Emma and thanks for being so nice about it Luke." Not sure whether to stay and chat or shuffle away. His eyes are amazing, so I just stare.

"That drink you necked looked pretty nasty." Luke picks up the glass and studies the disgusting remnants.

"Oh yes avoid the cement mixer with your life. It is a real bag of shite."

"I shall do that. I'm a beer kind of guy anyway or I do like a nice whiskey at the end of the night."

"Whiskey? Brrrr It gives me the shivers thinking about it. Are you an old man in disguise? Do you have a pair of slippers on down there?"

"I will have you know that whiskey is a man's drink not an old man's drink. You have to have a fine palette to appreciate it."

Luke pops his dinky up as he sips his beer, which makes us both laugh. I like him, he seems to have a good sense of humour.

"Not seen you around here before Luke, are you on holiday?"

"I'm competing for the first time in the Surf Fest competition. Have you heard of it?"

"Yes, I live around here so I know it is a tough competition. Hope you have your 'A' game, as the line up this year is impressive."

"I'm a huge fan of Billy Morth from California, so even if I don't do as expected I can at least catch him in fine form."

"Do you surf Emma?"

"No, I'm utterly crap." This makes him choke a little on his beer.

"You really have a way with words Emma."

"I'm better on a paddleboard. My brother is the surfer in the family. I'm going with him to watch it and my mum will have her catering van there too." I omit the part that I am going to be with James – not sure why I've left this out? Is it because Strictly Come Hottie is the first guy in bloody ages to approach me? Typical isn't it? I don't see any action for ages, then James expresses an interest now Luke is chatting me up. When you are not looking for something it really does come and bite you on the arse.

"The real question is Luke, are you any good at karaoke?"

"No, I'm utterly crap." He replies smirking at me.

"Well if you are staying here, you better get your ear plugs at the ready. As my lovely lady friends here will be belting out their tunes soon."

"Do you get up Emma?"

"I sure do." I reply striking my finest pose.

"Then I feel I have a reason to stay and enjoy the show."

Jen is in full flow singing Wham's Freedom. A couple of the girls are dancing behind pretending to be Pepsi and Shirley, it is so funny and the crowd is really behind them. Jen's notes are really squeaky, but she doesn't care and just carries on regardless. Luke is with his group chatting and enjoying the songs. You can see he knows the words and is singing along to Wham with Jen. We catch each other's eye and smile. As she finishes she does a bow to the whole bar (very ungracefully) and everyone cheers. She races down high on pure adrenalin and dives straight into my arms.

"Come on Em, choose your song and get your butt up there." Jen shouts, whilst embracing me with her sweaty body.

"Not sure what I want to sing. Too many choices." As I'm looking in the book the DJ announces the next person.

"Can we all welcome to the stage Joe, who will do a rendition of a famous Bon Jovi hit." I look up to the microphone and see bloody rubber lips ready to do a number. Great balls of bleeding fire, I am totally fixated. He looks like a rock star up there. You can see all the ladies nudging closer to the stage area to get a good old view of him. I just stand there – wide eyed and eager. He works the stage, swinging the microphone and hitting the notes well. Some of the girls have tried to stroke his legs and grab his shoes to get his attention. This man knows how to get a group of girls into a frenzy. I'm actually panting like a dog just watching the show. Jen and I just look at each other in disbelief. Jen never gets mesmerised by men, but I can see that she is gobsmacked too.

"Right Em, I've got the perfect song for you. Leave it to me." She grabs my form and heads towards the DJ." Oh shit, she could be choosing anything for me to sing. I could look a right pillock in front of Luke and rubber lips. I head to the bar for a cheeky sambucca before I get called. As the drink warms up my vocal chords, an arm reaches around my waist and swings me round.

"Hello there gorgeous. Do you have another one of those for me?" Joe places me down and turns my body to face him. His arm remains around my waist and he has pulled me towards him. "Wow, Emma you look stunning tonight." He looks me up and down, making my whole body turn beetroot red.

"Well done up there, you are a natural." I add pushing away a little. I'm struggling to breathe. He leans closer to the side of my face. His lips are touching my ear ever so gently. It's so erotic. I need an inhaler fast to open up my airways! Can't breathe.

"I love how your cheeks turn pick, when you get embarrassed Emma. Just like high school. You have not changed. Apart from growing into one sexy woman." Crikey, what is happening to my life? Where have all these men appeared from? And why all at once? Someone is ruddy testing me that's for sure. Nervously, I suck on my bottom lip and you can see Joe's eyes dart towards them. I know what is on his mind and it is on mine too. We never got to taste each other's lips at high school and by the look on his face, he wants it as much as I do.

"Next to the stage, everyone please welcome Emma." I feel Jen grab me away from Joe and push me towards the stage area. I feel a little unsteady and bewildered.

"That was good timing." Jen beams. "I don't think you want to be another cog on Joe's wheel. You can thank me later. Now go and get your groove on." Jen pushes me virtually onto the stage and I take a little stumble. I don't even know what I am singing. Although, Jen will know this and also knows that I can spot a tune from the first few chords. It is often a game we like to do together when we are chilling in her garden in the summer. A song will come on and we have to guess it the fastest. I normally win and Jen ends up making me something special for lunch. I often wonder if she may just let me win, so she doesn't have to taste my cooking. I listen carefully and wait patiently for it to start. I spot Luke moving closer to the stage on my left and he has a huge, gorgeous smile on his face. This makes me at ease. Then I look over to my right, Joe is coming closer to the stage, with such a naughty face on him. This makes me weak. I'm a mess. The song starts...I can't think with all these hormones whizzing around my body like a bleeding F1 racing car. I look at the screen and I can see the words start to appear. I know this song. Maybe if I just sing the days of the week and smile they won't really be bothered about what I'm singing. Let's Hear it For the Boys starts and images flash up in my mind. Wonderful memories of Jen. This was one of our favourite songs growing up and I would sing it to her to make her smile when she was fed up. I look into the crowd to see her and she raises her arms in the air with a cheer, whooping loudly in a supportive manner. I love that girl. I now need to do this song justice. I block out the crowd totally and grab the microphone. Let's do this. I used to love watching Whitney on the stage and marvelled at how she owned it. That is my plan and I start to strut up and down doing my thing. The group nearest the stage are singing along with me and this builds my confidence even more. I can see my lady friends standing on chairs and singing into their bottles. The security guards are on their way to tell them off, but I know they will not budge. They will probably end up on the chairs with the guards singing. I take a quick peek at Luke, who continues to smile and wave at me. Joe on the other hand has a group of girls around him, twerking and rubbing him up. It is so hot up here with the lights on me. I can feel the sweat building. I take off my cardigan and fling it into the crowd somewhere. As the song concludes I feel electric and happy endorphins are encouraging me to make it one hell of an ending. So I do and let rip. As the song ends, I look into the crowd to silence. Oh crap, was I that bad? As I place my microphone on the stand the whole place erupts with jubilation and applause.

"Sod the boys, everyone let's hear it for Emma." The DJ is also clapping and cheering. "Wow, you are one little minx. Same time next week?" He flashes me with a cheeky wink. I nod at him and float down the steps of the stage towards Jen.

"That's my girl, you were AMMMAAAZZZIINNGG." She grabs me and gives me a kiss on my cheek. "If James saw you do that. I am sure he would be whisking you off home right now!" Jen pokes me in the side.

"I think this belongs to you." Luke hands me my cardigan.

"Thank you, I got a bit lost in the moment. I would have been worrying about that later."

"So it is not part of your act then? You know like Elvis and his scarves. It's Emma and her cardi?" This make me laugh.

"I love Elvis, but no. Sorry I love that cardi. I can rub my sweat on something else for you, if you like? Your sleeve perhaps?" I pull his arm towards me in a joking manner.

"I can think of somewhere else you can put it?" Luke adds. I raise my eyebrows at his innuendo and turn pink.

"Would you like a nice cold beer buying? I think you deserve it after that. I can honestly say, I did not expect that or that side of you to emerge."

"Funny that, someone else said that same thing to me recently as well." My thoughts turn to James, I wonder how his night is going? Am I cheating on him, just by talking to these men? Then I stop myself, as we are not a couple yet, maybe never will be. I'm not doing anything wrong physically – in my mind maybe I am, but I'm not acting on my thoughts.

"Yes, Luke I would love one. Then do you fancy coming outside for some fresh air with me? It's a bit stuffy in here." I ask.

"Sure, I will be back in two minutes." Luke turns and heads to the bar, just as rubber lips swings me around and plants a big whopper of a kiss on my forehead.

"Shit Emma, you were hot. I mean on fire."

"I'm surprised you saw any of it. You looked otherwise occupied by your groupies."

"Oh Emma my love I saw it alright and I will be thinking of that performance for days to come." This comment slightly unnerves me and I can see exactly what Jen and my brother are saying. He is a player and no good for me. I can't get teased along and then dumped, my emotions couldn't take it. I decide to play along and get rid of him.

"I'd love to see you do another song, handsome. Pick something special for me." I rub my finger around his collar.

"You got it baby." He replies and heads over with haste to the DJ. He can't wait to get back up there. I quickly head outside before he sees me and I sit on the wall facing the ocean for a breather. I'm actually glad I don't get male attention – this is exhausting and I am missing out on having fun with Jen. My thoughts are interrupted – funny enough – by a man.

"I come baring drinks. Do you want company, or should I leave you to it?" Luke asks as he stands beside me. Nice of him to offer to leave. I like him more and more as the evening progresses.

"Please sit down. Thanks for the drink." I look at his own glass. "Are you on water, vodka or gin?" I ask.

"Water, my coach used to check on my alcohol levels when I started surfing comps. Then I just got used to not drinking much. I can stay out late; I just stop drinking beer after two or three bottles."

"I need a discipline like that. I'm drinking far too much at the moment." Luke moves closer to my side and we both look out to the blackness that is the sea. "I love living near the sea. It calms me and brings me back to normality. I can have the worst day at work, but then I return here and everything is okay in the world."

"I don't know what I would do if I wasn't near the sea. It's my sanity too. Talking about your sanity, was that flash git in there giving you trouble?" Luke is talking about rubber lips, he must have seen him.

"Now, he is a long story. A flash from the past I am glad I did not re-engage with shall we say."

"He looks truly besotted by you. I nearly left you to it, but I saw you escape out here alone and thought I should still honour you with a drink."

"Why thank you, kind sir. I appreciate it. Rubber lips..sorry I mean the flash git, known as Joe was in a bit of a love triangle with me at high school. Haven't seen him since then really. He turned up at my friend's house out of the blue and he just seemed fun. I seem to be lacking that element from my life, so I gravitate towards it whenever I can. Jen and my brother warned me to stay clear and they were right. They normally both are." I add with a sigh. "Anyhow, how are you feeling about the competition?" I ask in the hope of changing the subject.

"Nervous if I am honest. Not done this one before. Lots of smaller ones round the coast near me."

"How have you performed in them?"

"Good, top 5 in most. The more my confidence grows the more I take risks. This seems to score me more points."

"You should talk to my brother about it. He used to compete – knows most of the lads and could probably give you some tips." I offer, taking a nice long sip of the cold beer he has just brought me. I feel quite comfortable in his company. I don't feel like I have to prove something and be someone else. It is a refreshing feeling. "My mum owns the Cosy Cove Cafe; he will be in there in the morning after his surf. Just ask for Tom."

"Thanks Emma, that would be useful. I came out to tell you that I was heading back to the hotel. But I'd like to see you again?"

"That would be nice Luke, but just concentrate on your performance in the water! I will be watching and wishing you well from the beach."

"I shall take that as a maybe. Are you going to be okay on your own out here?"

"Oh yes, this is my town. I'm safe here. Probably head for a skinny dip with the ladies soon – part of our grand finale of the evening."

"Skinny dip? Here?" Luke seems to be lost for words. "Seriously?"

"Yes. Seriously. Now you run along and remember to ask for Tom tomorrow. I will tell him to look out for you. Good night Luke." I wave him off, just as the girls arrive outside. Luke turns round a couple of times as he heads further away. It is clear that he doesn't want to leave and miss the fun.

"Right ladies." I declare. "To the sea!" We all race towards the water a little further away from the bars and the crowd. We head close to the sand dunes and throw all our clothes off in a great big pile together. In fits of giggles and with just our skimpy knickers on we head into the sea. Not one of us has ever wanted to flash our lady bits after Jen told us that some fish can swim up your woo woo and stop you from pissing. Not sure if any of it is true? We feel the best protection is to just leave them on. The water is so chilly, but we quickly get used to it. We splash and laugh and try to run in the water towards each other to demonstrate our Dirty Dancing moves. We just end up landing on each other. It is so invigorating and funny.

Heading back to the dunes, I decide it is time to head home. Enough fun for one night and I don't fancy hyperthermia either. As I am pulling on my gear, I can hear some groaning coming from a dune. It sounds like someone is getting a good old seeing to! I tell myself to head in the opposite direction to grab a taxi, but something takes hold of my whole body and moves me towards the shenanigans. I feel possessed and very naughty. I tiptoe on the sand – like my normal walking would be heard. As I peer round I see a girl from the bar is getting jiggy with bleeding rubber lips! EWWW, Gross. I cover my eyes and turn to leave. The dirty git.

He told me he enjoyed some rumpy in the sand dunes. Didn't realise it was with anyone who would take an interest in him.

"Emma, Emma, wait. Have you come to join us?" Joe has spotted me.

"Not on your Nelly. I've had a lucky escape." I shout back and slide down the dune. It pains me to think that it could have been me there. What a fool I am. But a lucky fool, that I have people around me who protect me from Norberts like him. It has actually put a spring in my step as I head home. That was a close call.

Chapter
- Twelve -

Tom has headed out super early to surf this morning. Don't know how he does it? He ended up getting in during the early hours, not long after me. He brought the yummiest cheesy chips home with him and yes of course I helped him demolish them. What kind of sister would I be if I left him alone to enjoy them? Not a good one that is for sure. I wanted to ask all about James, but after my night of enlightenment and surprises I decided I didn't want any more drama to add to it. My brain just couldn't handle it.

I'm struggling to emerge from my pit. I've had a text message from Mum asking me to bob into the cafe. I haven't seen her since the party. I bet she thinks I'm avoiding her. I reply that I shall take a shower and see her soon. She sends me back lots of kisses, which makes me smile. I like it when she is like this i.e. being nice to me. Makes our relationship so much better than when she is being my 'mum' and questioning my judgement all the time. Suppose that's part of being a mum.

As I park up, I can see that it is a busy day at the cafe. Mum must be on a roaring trade with the build up to the Surf Fest competition. Hundreds of tourists stop by, especially to mum's place as it is where the main competitors take a break from the surf. It tickles me to watch all the girls sitting on the surrounding walls, acting all coy and giddy as their favourite surfer passes by. I used to be one of them, until I realised that nobody looked in my direction and I gave it up as a bad job to avoid humiliation. As I approach the cafe door I note that Tom's bright blue board is lined up, so he must be having breakfast inside.

There is not one table free as I enter. I can see Mum, with her beautiful rosy cheeks looking a little flustered behind the counter.
"Hi Mum, do you need some help?" I offer.
"Oh, Emma my dear. Yes that would be great." She embraces me with a kiss on my forehead and a quick

cuddle. "Can you jump on the till? I want to check on the orders?" Mum heads into the kitchen, I'm sure to add her own touch of culinary magic to the dishes. I add one of mum's Cosy Cove aprons to my waist and begin to serve. It really is hectic. Mum is mingling and serving, ensuring the quality of service is always of a high standard no matter how busy or quiet they are.

I spot Tom in the corner chatting to his group of friends. He comes alive when he returns home. A totally different Tom. Well this is classed as a holiday to him now, so I suppose that's what all holidays do to a person. They revive you and refresh you, making you all set to tackle the world back in normality. He waves as he spots me behind the counter and carries on talking. He is speaking to someone with their back to me. He points over to me and the mystery man turns around. It is Luke from last night. I had forgotten I had mentioned this place to him. I'm surprised that he took my advice and came to find my brother. He waves over at me – boy he looks just as good with ruffled damp hair and that same beaming smile from last night. Smiles like that are on my tick list. I noticed it last night in the bar. It is so handsome and broad; it makes you smile with him. My cheeks redden a little and I return to serving customers. Little did I know that Mum has caught our little exchange and she begins to smile like the cat who got the bloody whole van of cream.

"Who is that lovely man with Tom?" She asks.

"Which one Mum? There are a few of them over there." I add trying to dodge answering.

"You know Emma, the one who made you blush and gave you that twinkle in your eye. I have not seen that in some time." I bend down in the fridge to retrieve some milk and as I stand up, Luke is right in front of me.

"Hi Emma, nice to see you again and I am guessing you are Emma's mother? Nice to meet you, I'm Luke."

He extends his hand out to shake with my mum. She grabs the poor man and pulls him into a bear hug. I cringe all through my body.

"I'm Grace. Luke, it is a real pleasure to meet you. How do you know my gorgeous daughter?" Mum looks over to me with pure delight. She is planning my bleeding wedding, I just know it.

"We only met last night at a bar. I am competing in the Surf Fest and she recommended I speak with Tom about it here. By the way, this place is wicked. The food is delicious. If I didn't have to see my coach I would stay here all day." Comments like these will just make my mum love him even more. I smile and continue to serve.

"Are you working all day Emma?" Luke asks me.

"Oh, she doesn't work for her mum Luke, no she has just bobbed in to help me out. That's how kind and thoughtful she is. Did I mention also beautiful?" This makes Luke laugh. I decide to cut in.

"Right Mum, enough. Leave the poor man alone and stop trying to sell me. We have been through this before." I raise my eyebrows at her, but she really does not care. She's having a ball talking to Luke. In fact it has probably made her week.

"Grace, can I tell you a secret?" She nods but says nothing, like she is in a trance by him. Luke whispers "I am sold." It takes her a minute to realise that he is talking about me and I look at her also in amazement. Is he really saying that he is into me? Noooooo this cannot be. Even without his beer goggles on? But to be fair he didn't drink too much at all last night. I distract myself by cutting some cake, as I am not sure how to react to this. Mum on the other hand is doing her own River Dance around the cafe.

"Emma, if you are free tonight I am just hanging out in The Edge Hotel. If not we can meet up after the competition?"

"She would love to do both." Mum replies.

"Mum! Give it a rest. Thanks Luke I will see what plans Tom has for later."

"Here's my number." He writes it on a napkin and heads out. "Nice to meet you Grace, hope to see you tomorrow at the competition."

"Oh yes Luke, I will be cheering you on that's for sure." Mum bellows out as he leaves.

"Well, if you don't want that hunk of a man. I'm sure your Dad will let me add him to my celebrity snog list. He is yum."

"Mum, I hope you are joking?" I ask in disgust. Who wants to know that their Mum has this kind of list with your Dad? Not I!

"Thanks for your help Emma, go and sit with your brother and I will bring you some treats over as a thank you." Mum whisks the apron off me and heads into the kitchen singing merrily away to herself.

"Morning sis, how are you feeling?" Tom enquires. I plonk myself down next to him and help myself to a sip of his brew. "Please help yourself." He jokes.

"Remember brother what's yours is mine and what's mine is mine." This makes him smile as it was something I used to say to him when we were younger. I hated sharing my stuff with him, but Mum always made him share his stuff with me – because he was older. The younger siblings always play on this, well I certainly did and still do today. Mum heads over with my own cuppa and an egg and sausage bap. "Thanks Mum that looks divine." I slice into the bap and the juicy egg flows everywhere. I start to devour this little piece of heaven. Dipping my bap in the egg yolk that escaped.

"Emma, do you know you are totally disgusting? Don't ever let any other man see you eat like that." I just pout my mucky lips at him and continue to munch. I don't care what I look like in front of Tom.

"So Tom, you didn't tell me how your night with James went."

"You can ask him yourself." Tom points to the doorway as James breezes through looking fresh and vibrant. He has a tigger bounce in his step as he notices us on the other side of the cafe. Shit, I shove the rest of the bap in my mouth and munch as quick as I can before he reaches the table. My brother points to the corner of my mouth, so I wipe any evidence of my juicy bap away quickly. He puts a thumb up to say all is good, as James arrives at the table.

"Morning all, can I join you?" James asks as he places his hand on the back of my shoulder. This sends a jolt across my body. It lingers there a while longer and he gives it a little affectionate squeeze. "How are you Emma? Not seen you for a couple of days. Are you missing me?" James asks giving me a wink. Tom nearly chokes on his brew watching his friend crack on to me. I want to know what the fecking Nora he has had for his breakfast? Alright, Jeremy Beadle jump the hell on out from where you are hiding. The men around me have gone totally mad. Are they taking the piss out of me? Poor Emma, let's pretend we like her and then let her fall flat on her face as we dump her. This has been the story of my life with men, so why would now be any different?

"So James, Emma was just asking me how our night was? How would you describe it James?" James looks at

Tom very awkwardly and doesn't answer. What are they trying to say to each other? I grab my cuppa for protection and I hold on tightly to see how this plays out. "What's going on?" I ask giving them both a very probing and an 'I'm not happy with what is going on here' stare. James finally answers.

"It was very quiet. We just had a good catch up, a few too many beers and...well that was it." James replies nervously adding his hand again to my shoulder in some sort of reassuring manner. Mum appears next to me looking at James's hand. Her eyes just continue to widen. James removes his hand quickly and his face reddens. She is going to have a ruddy field day with this. I need to finish up and get out of here as quickly as humanly possible.

"Hello James, so nice to see you. I believe you and Tom had fun last night. A few of the locals informed me of your antics."

"Quiet huh?" I respond moving my chair a little further away from James, who seems to be lying to me. My brother on the other hand is in a whole pile of crap. Wait till I get him on his own. How is it that my mother knows what they have been up to?

"Do you want your usual cappuccino James?" Mum asks.

"Thanks Grace, a large one and a teacake please." James looks over to me, but I divert my eyes sharply in another direction. I remember what James told me about seeing Tom again – he wanted some lady advice. So, he must have got the advice, received the attention and now I'm just one of his many ladies. Knew this would sodding happen.

"I don't think our night was quite as dramatic as yours Emma. Luke told me some interesting information." I just look at Tom with no words. What has he told him? Tom likes to do this and get lots of information out of me, when really he knows nothing.

"Who is Luke?" James asks.

"It was very quiet. The girls chatted, had a few too many beers, shots and gins. That was it. No story to write home about." I reply hastily ignoring James's question.

"So there were no solo performances?" Tom asks.

"I may have sung a song." I add matter of factly – nothing he can get me on there.

"So rubber lips didn't try to come onto you?" I can't believe Tom is asking me this. Here and now in front of James.

"No, he was just being friendly and he had plenty of female attention. He just didn't have my attention."

"Who the hell is rubber lips?" James asks.

"So you didn't go skinny dipping at the end of the night either?" Holy shit – he has told him everything and Luke has probably seen everything. The git. The pervert. How dare he tell my brother stuff from my night out. He has only just met me and he is judging me.

"Skinny dipping? Rubber who? And who the fuck is Luke?" James shouts in a very high pitched tone.

He appears to be extremely pissed off. Well, good because that is how he just got me to feel. Right back at ya!

"Well at least you both know the highlights of my night, but can't come to share any of yours. Well, right now I am not interested. Hope you got off with as many women as possible. I don't care." I stand up to leave and head towards the door. My mum stops me before I leave.

"Emma, it seems that you have the interest of two fine fellows. Now choose wisely and be careful. But just so you know, I am very proud of you."

"No mum, no men on the go. I don't trust the slimy gits. I am better off alone. See you later." I head out before she can stop me. How can she be proud of that? Of all the things I do in life, finding a man wins me my mum's approval. Go bleeding figure! Well I am going to go home to freshen up then head over to see Luke later and give him a piece of my mind. The cheeky sod, does he not know the code? What goes on during a night out (without your brother) stays on a night out. Not very catchy I know, but you get the gist. I am not a happy bunny. I am acting like a petulant teenager and I don't sodding care. I've had a few missed calls from James, with messages that we need to talk. NOW the sod wants to talk! What – to brag about the other women my so called brother has helped him connect with last night? I am not in the mood at all. My brain even hurts from the constant scowling and grimacing torturing myself and thinking about what James got up to. I find Baby I Don't Care on my phone and blast it out. This song seems to be good for many occasions and uplifting of my current shite mood.

Looking in the mirror I have scrubbed up pretty well. I've put some skinny jeans on, which accentuate my bottom and a nice crisp, white shirt. I add some make up, only a bit as I don't use much. But I add my eye liner to make my eyes pop out and say 'don't piss with me, I'm in a shit mood and I won't take any crap' – bet you didn't know make up could say that? Well mine can and it will tonight as I take on Lukey boy. I decide to walk over to The Edge Hotel, it's not too far and the fresh air will do me a world of good. Blow away the cobwebs, so to speak.

The hotel is all lit up and residents are sat out enjoying the evening. It is not too chilly, the summer is coming and you can feel the warmth begin to stir around us. I head inside and spy Luke sat alone, deep in thought at the front bay window which overlooks the sea. The funny thing is, the anger that nearly blew my top off has diminished seeing him and I realise that I don't want to shout and ball at him at all. He seems a really nice and genuine guy and he had my mum eating out of the palm of his hand. I don't want to mess with his head before the competition. What was I thinking? This was a mistake. I turn to head home.

"Emma? Is that you?" In my head I want to ignore him and keep on walking, but I turn and smile. I don't want to be rude, that is not in my nature. "Where are you going? Have you changed your mind?" Wow, lots of questions take me by surprise. I decide the best course of action is to lie...sorry mother.

"I was just looking for you Luke, didn't realise that was you sat there." I don't think he believed me, but he got up anyway and gave me a delicate kiss on my cheek. It really made the whole of my insides purr.

"Come and sit with me, think I got the best seats in the house." He gestures to the window and the absolutely beautiful silhouette of the coast. It is just magnificent – why have I never been in here to see this before? All the street lights are twinkling and it is just perfect. As I sit down a waiter appears.

"Would you like to see the menu or just order a drink from the bar?" The waiter asks.

"Can I have a pint of whatever you have on draft please and what do you fancy Emma?"

"Can I have the same as what he is having? Thank you." I reply.

"You drink pints as well Emma? Most impressive. Thanks again for offering Tom's time this morning. He really is a great guy. He has invited me back for a night out when my competition is over."

"I am sure he will introduce you to all the talent in the area. Tom is very good at that." I add bitterly. Luke doesn't seem to pick up on my nasty(ish) comment.

"He certainly thinks a lot about you. You seem to have a very close relationship with your family." The waiter pops our drinks down and a couple of pots of nibbles. Perfect for when you are nervous.

"It's nice to have him home, not sure when he will be back though. So you may be waiting some time for your night out with him." I shove a whole load of Bombay mix into my mouth.

"Maybe you could show me around then, think I would prefer that." He adds giving me the most delicious look over his pint glass. My heart begins to thump. "Tom was asking me plenty of questions about your night out.

Sorry if I dropped you in it." There we have it the bloody elephant in the room.

"Yes, he did mention that he knew about various events of last night." I remain cool and calm. "Somehow he knew about the skinny dipping. Did you leave last night or stay to enjoy the show?" As I look at him, he smirks. I have my answer right there. He stayed! "Did you enjoy what you saw?" I ask smiling at him now.

"Mighty fine. Not laughed that much in ages. Especially when you threw your naked body on your friend and you both just landed on your backs in the sea."

"Oh yes that was our Baby and Jonny move. I have to be Jonny now and lift Jen. She has done her back in from lifting me. For a little thing she has super strength. Didn't you fancy coming and joining us?"

"Think my bits would have shrivelled up into prunes if I went in the sea without my wetsuit on. For a surfer I'm pretty crap when it comes to the cold."

"You and me both." I add laughing "We have something in common there. You are lucky that I don't have my bed socks on right now, I can feel them getting chilly and I'm a right nowty cow when I'm cold."

"Emma you are a real catch, do you sit at home in your PJs, wrapped in a blanket, drinking ale and watching romantic stuff?"

"You are spying on me Luke. I will need to get a restraining order on you! Just for the record it is mainly a cup of tea and a packet of biscuits. Did you stay to see what happened when I got out of the sea?"

"No, I didn't perve on you getting dressed if that's what you are thinking. Although, now I wished I had. Why? What else did you get up to?" He asks, clearly intrigued.

"Remember the guy from the bar, the Bon Jovi wannabe?" Luke nods. "Well I heard some noises in the dune and he was there getting his end away with one of the girls from the bar."

"Did you see?" Luke asks clearly intrigued.

"Oh yes, I saw everything. Then the cheeky bleeder saw me and asked me to join. The nerve." I shake my head in disgust.

"Does your brother know this? I'm only asking, because I think he would go ape on him."

"As much as I would have thoroughly enjoyed watching that. No he doesn't know and you my friend are not to mention anymore to him. You've told him enough. He thinks I am his sweet, younger sister. Don't want to spoil his illusion of me." It did cross my mind to chastise him, but I am no longer the angry bird and I am enjoying his company.

"No problem and I'm sorry again for sharing the other stuff. He's such a great guy and I felt like telling him all sorts of stuff. Not sure what came over me."

"Oh I do, he has real charm and is handsome as hell. He can get whatever he wants. But he is such a nice, honest guy and people tell him all sorts. It's been good for his job when he is reporting. He can find out some juicy stuff just by fluttering those big eyes. Men and women alike fall for him."

"Yes, I saw that on the beach. Plenty of girls hanging around waiting for his attention." Luke looks out of the window thoughtfully.

"I'm sure some were there for you too Luke."

"That's flattering of you to say but I'm not that kind of guy. The groupies that come with surfing, is not my thing. They are just attracted to the competition and being in the lime light. I surf, because I love it and the competitions are a bonus. I want to meet someone who gets that. Do you fancy going out properly on a ...date with me sometime?"

"Out where?" I ask feeling nervous at his question.

"Hitting the waves." He adds quickly.

"Oh yeah, sure. I will get my paddleboard and watch you from afar. Maybe I could take you out with me and the paddleboard – but be wary it can be extreme and wild. It will blow your mind."

"Yeah I'd like that. It's such a beautiful area to explore. After the competition we can set something up. Tell your Tom I'm sorry, but I have received a better offer."

"Don't think anyone has chosen me over Tom before. This is a very proud moment. One to cherish and remember."

"Cheers to memories. Let there be many more." Luke raises his empty glass.

"Here's to you doing well in the Surf Fest. I will be sat eating my mum's sausage baps and cheering you on."

"I'm starving Emma, do you fancy sharing some snacks from the bar?" Luke picks up the menu and starts to read out the bar snacks. "We could share nachos? Cheesy garlic bread? Cheese board? Halloumi fries? Yorkshire pudding wrap?"

"Yes, yes, yes to them all Luke! I am positively salivating here." Luke waves over the bar man and asks for one of everything from the snacks menu and orders a pot of tea for two. This is my kind of man. Makes a decision, makes me happy and knocks my socks off in the process. I suppress images of James from my mind and enjoy my evening eating, laughing and sharing my night with a very intelligent and handsome man. Moments like this do not happen often. I intend to enjoy every minute.

Chapter
- Thirteen -

I hear a door click shut and begrudgingly stir from such a deep wonderful sleep. The sun is just beginning to peek in the room and bring forth a new day. I can hear the heating come on, which I love because I know the room is going to become cosy and snugly very soon. As I turn over to return to the land of slumber, the noises from the radiator start to concern me. That is not the sound my radiators make. I don't recognise that sound at all. In a panic I bolt up worried that someone is in my apartment. Looking around it becomes very apparent that I did not make it back to my apartment last night...I spent the night with Luke. I am in his hotel room. Oh dear lord, this is not like me. What was I thinking? What did we do? I've not done the dirty deed in such a long time. I must have been awful, as he has left before I woke up. I put my hands to my face in shame and lean back onto the pillows. I am a fool. A man shows me the slightest bit of interest and I am a sucker to being used. As I lie back I feel a piece of paper crunch behind my head. On the front it says 'To Sleepy Head'. As I open it I scan to the bottom to read 'See you soon Luke'. I then realise that he has not bolted and continue to read it properly.

Good Morning

Thank you for last night. It has been a long time since I chatted all night with a girl and kept my interest. I have headed to the gym before my competition starts. Before you freak out – you fell asleep on the armchair down by the bar. I tried to wake you up, but you told me you wanted to stay. Hope you don't mind I carried you upstairs. You then fell onto my bed and snored all night, fully clothed. I did want my bed back and I tried to put you on the sofa, but you would not budge. I think that deserves a back massage, because the sofa was shit – you were right to stay on the bed ☺. Hope to see you later at the beach, stay and enjoy some breakfast, the pancakes are delicious. See you soon Luke

P.S Sorry about your head, you are pretty heavy for a small thing, I banged it on the door trying to find my room key.

I feel the top of my head and there sure is a sore bump there. He must have given it a right whack. But I was too knackered to even wake up from that. Pathetic. He is very chivalrous – carrying me to the room, allowing me to stay in the bed when it could come at a cost for him and his competition. I'm so selfish. I should have left and let him get some rest. He was probably being too polite to tell me to shove off. However, thinking back to last night, it only brings a huge daft smile to my face. This man has come out of the blue and put me in the most wonderful and uplifting mood. Isn't it funny how things turn out? I arrived to give him the wrath of Emma and we ended up talking in the bar until the early hours drinking tea and reminiscing. Luke is like another Jen. He is so easy to talk to and I don't feel like I need to molly coddle him and say anything to make him feel better about himself. But he is leaving soon and even though I don't want to admit it, something is kind of going on with James. If you count a snog and texting a relationship? No, I am putting too much pressure on myself to act in a certain way. It hasn't worked out so far for me, so I'm going with the bleeding flow. Luke is as sexy as hell. James is a hunk of burnin' love. Let's see where the tide takes me? I lie back and plan how I am going to see this through without hurting anyone, but sussing out which man is right for me. I'd like a piece of both pies but I need to be careful I don't get burnt in the process.

Chapter
- Fourteen -

After a huge pile of pancakes with maple syrup and bacon I waddle back home to get showered and changed. I feel like I am doing the walk of shame back to my apartment. As I pass the local fishermen heading out, I am expecting them to be whispering about me wearing the same clothes from last night. I pick my pace up and get in doors before I blush anymore and combust.

Heading to the shower I bluetooth a bit of 'Boston' onto the sound system, a cracking tune to continue my good mood and get the morning started. As I'm doing a little air guitar in the steamy bathroom a pink piece of paper slides under my door. Another bloody note. What is going on? Is Luke here now? I open it to see my brother's writing.

To my dippy younger sister.

Please stop wallowing in self-pity and come out of your pit and have a brew with me. I haven't seen you all night – you wouldn't open your door to me. I think you have it all wrong about my night out with James. Let me explain before you ruin things with James..and me. I know you over-think stuff. Move your butt, before I come in there and get you out myself.

Love Tom

P.S Right now! Xxx

Oh boy, Tom thinks I have been in my room all night feeling sorry for myself. How wrong can he be? Maybe I should tell him that his naughty little sister has been out all night and has only just come in. In the words of Bobby Brown 'Two can play that bleeding game'. It is normally him showering after a night of getting his leg over with a lady and leaving them before they wake up. Well, to be fair he hasn't done it recently – in fact apart from Poppy he hasn't shown any interest in the ladies at all. With Poppy the affection being all one sided on her part. I need to speak with him and find out what is going on. I wrap the towels around my body and open the door. Tom is there holding a big mug of tea and a pile of crumpets.

"Come on sis, follow me." He heads into the living room, where the World Strongest Man is on the telly. The biggest smile hits my face – I love this programme. "I recorded this last night for us to watch together. I remembered how much we used to watch this when Mum and Dad would go out. Do you remember, we would get our sleeping bags on the sofa and stuff our faces watching it? I have happy memories of this too you know."

"Oh Tom, I do remember and it brings back warm fuzzy feelings. I also remember you banging on Robocop as well when Mum and Dad weren't there – I also loved that!" We laugh together and sit side by side mesmerised by the power of these mighty men.

"Do you remember the night Mum and Dad came back from a Christmas party and Dad was that sozzled he fell into the tree and he got caught in the lights. There was an almighty crash and he had landed on the floor with the tree by his side."

"Yes I do, I remember how furious Mum was that he actually fell asleep on the floor next to the tree and didn't move until the next morning. We found it hilarious. Mum left us to it and she stormed upstairs. We carried on watching Rambo. I miss times like that. Have you anymore thoughts about moving back?" I ask hopefully.

"Yes, in fact the night I went out with James he offered me a job with him. He is looking at doing boat tours off the coast and we stop at different destinations and cook for guests using local produce. He and Bobby want to expand and offered me a slice of the action as a partner."

"Wow, Tom that sounds amazing and very generous of James to offer that to you. I know how precious he is about the family business." I reply extremely surprised.

"What do you think you will do?"

"I said I would have a good think about it. I would need to put some collateral in, but my London flat could be that – if the offer to stay with you for a while is still on the table?" Tom pouts at me and bats his gorgeous big eyes. This news is the best I have heard in such a long time. I jump on Tom and give him a huge cuddle.

"You have to say yes! It is the change you wanted and you know I love having you here. You can stay for as long as you need. This makes me so happy Tom, I can't tell you." I sit back down bouncing on the sofa with happiness.

"Well, I would need to sell pretty soon and hand my notice in."

"I think it sounds like you have made up your mind Tom?"

"Yes, I think you are right. It looks like I am moving back home."

"Yes, yes, yes." I scream at the top of my lungs. "He's coming home, he's coming Tom is coming home!" I sing happily to him. "Mum and Dad are going to be ecstatic. When are you telling them?"

"I will mention it before I get on the train. Haha that will freak them out and then they will pester you for all the answers, as I wave bye to you all."

"Oh cheers brother, maybe I will rethink the offer of you staying with me after all if you are going to do things like that to me. I forgot how cruel you are!"

"Right, now that my move back has been sorted I want to speak with you about how you reacted at Mum's cafe yesterday." I just shrug. I actually don't want to talk about it.

"Like I said I'm happy that you both found some lady friends to keep you company. I just didn't want to hear about it from Mum. I was beginning to like James – the swine."

"Emma, your mind really does baffle me. You really need to listen to me as I will only say this once. It's not good for my street cred. Are you listening?" I just look at him a little baffled. "Okay, we made it into four of our finest locals; pub number one we tried a few of the new ales on cask and talked about my disastrous relationship with Lucy as we sat next to a log fire. Pub number two, we ordered fish and chips and sipped on a couple of gins. Rhubarb is currently my favourite! Pub number three we bought a pad from the shop and sat planning out the business venture and how I could be part of it. We took over a table for ten people and there were papers and pint glasses all over it. Finally, pub number four we had a couple of whiskeys and took on the ladies darts team in a match. To which the 70 year old ladies won and we had to buy them drinks all night. James and I drowned our sorrows in a whiskey bottle and headed home. Rock and roll!" The look on my face says it all.

"So James didn't get tips off you for wooing the opposite sex?" I ask.

"No, Emma. The only tips he got were about you and what you like to do. I think he has it bad for you. But you know James; he keeps his cards close to his chest. He is great at getting what he wants in business, but not in relationships. He hasn't been with anyone and I think he is worried on how best to handle you and keep you interested." This news floors me. I have been an idiot. I have been flirting with James, flirting with Luke and the one thing he asked me to do about not hurting him could be what I end up doing. All because I got my facts wrong and didn't listen. How old am I? Why do I continue to make idiotic choices and ruin good things? The one good thing out of all of this is I do like James, I think Luke is just gorgeous but I couldn't see a future with him. I realised that when I woke up in his room and felt sick at the thought of having rumpy with him. I was imagining that it was James coming into the room serving me pancakes. "Right, now you know it is up to you to make the right choice for you. Now get your stuff together we need to head to help Mum at Surf Fest." Tom pulls me off the sofa and we head to the beach for some surfing action.

Chapter
- Fifteen -

Parketh beach is not far from Mum's cafe. It is just breathtaking and gobsmacks me by its beauty every time I look at it. The only problem today is that it is full of visitors taking over and spoiling the scene. I know it is good economically for the area, but I still want the beach just to be for a small number of people. There are lots of girls wearing basically next to nothing, flashing their bits to the male competitors. I feel overdressed in my shorts and sweatshirt.

We head over to the World Surf League competition board to see the format of the morning. I spy Luke's name in the heats and this makes me feel all sorts of funny emotions. Excited to watch him in action, nervous to see him again after last night and part of me wants to run a mile from any complications. It seems that Luke is doing well with his points from the competitions and he is moving up the rankings – very impressive. It is then that I notice that Tom is looking at me with real confusion on his face.

"The faces you pull sis are so attractive. Something is definitely on your mind. Are you ready to tell me yet?" Tom just stands staring at me for an answer, but I truly do not know where to start. "Is it James?" He enquires.

"I'm just a little confused at the moment. I'm afraid of hurting anyone – me most of all. But I finally want to enjoy being with somebody. Nobody has shown one bit of teeny weeny interest in me for well...a bloody long time and now it's like buses all coming along a once." I rant at poor Tom.

"Is this to do with the surf lad Luke?" Tom interrupts.

"Yes." I shout not meaning to. "My brain is struggling, it's gone into overdrive and you know I can't cope when it does that! Let's head over to Mum and get busy. This will help me forget about my woos for now."

"Okay, if you are sure?" Tom asks and I just nod a little defeated and glum. I link Tom's arm and we set off. The sand is so cool between my toes and the soft texture caressing my feet begins to edge away my troubles. To be fair in the grand scheme of life they shouldn't be classed as 'troubles'.

"Tom? Is that you?" A guy's voice shouts behind us.

As we both turn we are face to face with what can only be described as an Adonis, a Hercules of the surf...it's bloody Aquaman in the flesh! "Tom, long time no see mate."

"Billy, how the hell are you?" They both engulf each other in a big grizzly bear hug. I just stand there mesmerized. I start by taking in his strong, tanned feet. Working up to his thighs, which look like they could crack anything open. Moving on up to his solid, grind me anywhere hips. Finally, to his broad- rippling abs and chest. His short, blond hair is wet and spiked. Can I ruffle my hands in there? Would that be considered rude as we have only just met? Am I dribbling? I dab the sides of my mouth quickly just encase.

"And who is this fine lady?" He extends his hand out for me to shake. I take his hand, but cannot speak.

"This is my sister, Emma. Emma this is Billy Morth from California. Probably gonna beat everybody's arses out of the water today, eh Billy?" Is that a mischievous twinkle I spy in this godly man's blue eyes? I like it.

"I'm certainly going to try my best." He replies still holding my hand and his thumb is stroking my hand. All sorts of explosions are occurring in my body, it's like the bleeding 4th of July.

"What are the conditions like today?" Tom asks Billy.

"Clean surf, just got to keep an eye on the 'offshore wind' other than that I don't think we could ask for better conditions. Not fancy getting back in the game Tom – you were pretty good in your time." This makes Tom laugh.

"Hey mate, I'm not that old. Could probably struggle getting a score of 3.9 now. I'd be lucky. Only went out the other morning, not been able to get out for a long time. Still have the bug though."

"Do you surf Emma?" He finally releases my hand, but I don't want him to. I spy a little smirk on his lips, as I remain holding on. Cocky git. Don't fall for it Emma – I chant to myself. It will end in pain. What about James and Luke? My conscience sparks up. Who are they again? My naughty side responds. Oh boy, I'm all of a fluster.

"No, I go out on my paddleboard or kayaking with my dad. Much more relaxing for me. Plus I am rubbish on a surf board." I reply shyly, smiling coyly at Billy.

"Well if you had a real instructor." Billy says pointing at himself. "I am sure you'd be a pro before long."

"Yeah, yeah." Tom interrupts.

"Well I had better head off. It's been a real pleasure to meet you Emma. It'd be great to catch up after the comp Tom – hope you are both staying around."

"Good luck Billy, we are helping Mum out just over there." Tom points to Mum's Airstream Bambi Van.

"Is your mum Grace?" We both nod. "Aww she has been down here from early doors feeding and watering us. She's real cracker. I know where you get your good looks from Emma." Billy says with a wink and heads towards the water. "See you both later." With that the Adonis turns and heads away. My feet are stuck firmly in the sand watching his tight buns bounce off into the distance. Ooh how I'd like to take a big bite of that delightful tush.

"Come on Emma, let's go before you create another ocean with your drool!" Tom jokes laughing at me.

I punch him in his arm. "Funny." I declare rather too loudly, as Billy whips round to see me still glued to the spot.

As we arrive at Mum's van she is very busy whipping together her famous smoothies. They are delicious full of vitality and energy.

"Jump aboard you two, it's going to be a busy old day!" Mum is in really good spirits, bouncing around singing as she serves, cooks and smiles all that the same time. "Em, my lovely girl can you do the drinks order? Tom can you set yourself up on the till and I shall do whatever cooking is needed. My smoothie recipes are at the back of the blender if you need them Em, but I am sure you know them by now."

"I sure do Mum and I am going to make myself a banana and honey bad boy to get my day started." I take a look at Mum's menu for the event. It can only be described as heaven. There are avocado bruschettas, stacks of pancakes with fruit or bacon, Belgian waffles, various fresh sandwiches and a range of burgers all served with skinny fries or sweet potato fries. I have decided to stay here all day and try them all out. I can see Tom has a similar idea, he is currently shovelling in a pile of pancakes with berries and ice cream.

As I am putting together a cappuccino and a macchiato for a customer I spy James and Bobby's butty van a short distance away. In fact, I smelt it before I spy him serving one of his famous sausage butties to a gorgeous brunette. The queue at his van is humungous; it's giving my mum's van a run for its money. The queue is mainly of girls, probably only waiting to get a smile off the gorgeous James. Ooh my ugly jealous head is beginning to appear. I didn't realise James was working today. Seems like we have all been roped into to doing our bit. Looking around the beach, the crowd and excitement is definitely building. Our local radio station is presenting the day and it is already rocking out some crackers to fire the crowd and competitors up. There are many stalls and vans now set up selling an array of food, drinks and the latest beach gear. The prices are ranked right up, I'd have to sell a kidney for some ruddy shorts. It is a good time to sell, especially when the young ones have had a few bevies at lunchtime. They seem to whip out their wallets willy nilly. Don't know how they manage to afford the stuff. I only just survived at college with my part-time job. Nowadays they can afford all the latest gear, fashion and holidays. I was lucky if I could muster together money to make a pasta bake and a bottle of Hock. I actually still can't afford to deck myself out in new fashionable gear – what am I doing wrong? I take another peek at Tom's van and there is a brazen hussie appearing to be giving him a piece of paper...it must be her bloody number. My blood is boiling and ready to explode. How dare he accept it? Why didn't he just push her away and say get lost? I just don't get men.

"I won't need you two much longer." Mum bellows across the van. I've got help arriving soon from my staff. You can both enjoy the festival. I may pop out soon and watch Billy and Luke in their heats." Mum winks at me cheekily. "I met Billy this morning, he's a right one. Knows how to sweep an old lady off her feet that one does. If I was 20 years younger boy we would have fun." "EWWW Mum please stop." I ask putting my hands over my ears. "That thought is doing all the wrong things to my brain." I move away from her to get some space from the randy woman.

"Morning Grace, can I have a Super Smoothie please?"

"Hi Luke, nice to see you again." Mum replies with a beaming smile on her face – here she goes again. I nudge Mum in an attempt to tell her that I am not here. I sink slowly to the van floor. Tom is looking at me in bewilderment.

"Do you want a large or medium one Luke?"

"Medium please, thanks Grace. Have you seen Emma arrive yet? I was wondering if she was still eating all the pancakes at the hotel when I left her this morning." With that comment Mum and Tom look straight in my direction with such shock and surprise it makes me get the nervous giggles. I try to get up to make Luke's smoothie but I end up landing back down on the floor crying and laughing silently. I press the tea towel into my face to try and stop, but I think their faces just knocked me over the edge. Tom sees the funny side of things and kicks me in my side to move over. He makes the smoothie and hands it over to Luke.

"Good luck today, Luke. Spoke with Billy before he said conditions are looking good. Hopefully Emma will be here soon, so we can watch you."

"Thanks Tom, I will catch up with you both later. Thanks Grace. See you again." They both say their goodbyes to Luke and promptly turn to look at me.

"Spill!" Mum declares. When I have calmed myself down I proceed to tell them about my night with Luke, about my conflict between Luke and James. How I thought James was doing the dirty on me. I also confess my lust for the new Billy. Sod it I thought they need to know it all.

"Now I understand why you looked so confused this morning Emma. You should have just told me. But trust me when I say from experience, men do not want to be messed about and they certainly do not want to think they are competing for your affection. You can't play them along. You know that James has declared he likes you and does not want you to hurt him. Luke obviously is smitten with you. I saw the way Billy was mentally undressing you. You need to decide what you want and stick with it." Tom shares his words of wisdom and both me and mum stop what we are doing and listen. He knows from his experience with Lucy and I don't want him to think I am like her? Am I? Am I constantly waiting for something better to come along? I would never survive in a relationship if that is the case.

"Was he mentally undressing me?" I ask.

"Emma! Concentrate on what I have just said. I'm definitely not diving into anything new at the moment. Lucy was enough for any man to endure."

"I'm sorry love, we haven't had time to talk about this. Didn't realise it affected you so much." Mum rubs Tom's arm.

"Well it has and I don't want to see Emma make the same mistakes that she did." This comments actually hurt me.

"How dare you Tom. I am not like her. I have not had a real relationship with anyone to make that mistake. I have two maybe three men finally interested in me and not because my mum has asked them to go on a date with me. They like me and it is refreshing and new and it is what I dream about each night. I go to sleep dreaming I am Vivian Ward from Pretty Woman or Allie Hamilton from the Notebook. I want to be the one kissing in the rain, taking long leisurely strolls at dusk hand in hand. My woolie bed socks and tartan pjs are just not cutting it without someone to snuggle up to and love me for me."

"Life is not movie or a romantic scene from a novel Emma, you need to grow up and realise people can get hurt from these emotions." With that Tom puts down his apron and heads out of the van. Luckily, two members of Mum's staff have turned up to take over.

"I will leave you to it too Mum. See you later." I don't even wait for a reply. I feel very low, stupid and naive. I leave the van as swiftly as possible with tears prickling my eyes. I need to go somewhere out of the way of people. I run over the dunes further down the beach away from the competition and cry. Nobody is around to ask me if I am okay and I am glad about this. I don't want anybody's sympathy. Tom was right in some ways, I can't play these lovely men along and I do need to grow up in some respects. I've just never seemed to get it right. From high school and present day. I am looking for too much in a man and nobody is good enough. But that isn't true. James I have adored from afar for many years and now he is interested I'm running for the hills. Luke is new, fresh and likes me for me. I've never talked to anyone and enjoyed their company so much. Billy is just bleeding well hot and would only be a one night pony for any woman. He would be moving on like a shot. Not relationship potential. I start to sing 'You've lost that loving feeling' to myself, alone on the dunes. Because that is it...it's gone, gone, gone...woohoooo. I lie back, close my eyes and belt it out.

"It surely can't be Righteous Brothers bad?"

It's Jen. I sit up and she snuggles next to me giving me the best cuddle I have had in ages. In fact since the morning we woke up in bed together.

"I've just seen Tom. He's told me what's going on. He's worried he has shouted at you." Jen shares.

I just nod, lie back down and continue to sing. Jen doesn't push it; she gets beside me, holds my hand and sings along with me. Tears are falling down the sides of my face and I just let them roll. Friend therapy and singing was just what was needed. She doesn't judge me out loud and I appreciate that. I can tell what she is saying to me in her mind and it goes along the lines of 'get up you dick, sort this out and move on'.

"Thanks Jen." I wipe my face and sit up. "Your advice is just what I needed."

"What? I haven't given you any advice." Jen looks confused.

"No and thank you for not putting judgement on me, but I imagined what you would say and I appreciate that."

"Well, you are welcome for whatever I offered and I hope it helps. PS can I have my friend back soon? I haven't seen her in a while and Ava is missing her auntie Em." I nod.

"Can we go and watch the competition together a little away from the crowd? I don't want to miss it." I ask.

"Sure, get your bum up, dust yourself off and get on with life. This is just a stumbling block. Don't be so hard on yourself, you are not used to this Em. I'm proud you've finally put yourself out there." Jen holds her hand for me to take.

"That was kind of what I expected you to say, apart from maybe calling me a dick." I smile at her.

"Oh boy, I totally forgot that – yes you really are a dick."

"Much better, thanks Jen. Let's go and see how everyone is doing." We run with great speed down the sand dunes together laughing. I don't have a plan, but I have a good feeling that I am on the right track to resolving it.

I take some deck chairs from Mum's van and set us up just behind the main crowd. There are massive screens up around us, so we wouldn't miss any of the action being further back. Jen has brought some tubs of ice cream and a blanket each to snuggle into. True friendship! It's not cold, but you know how I feel about a blanket and a snuggle. My idea of heaven. The radio station's speakers are blasting out Reef's 'Put your hands up'. This tune alone perks a woman right up. I sit happily with my best friend tapping along and munching on honeycomb scrumdiddilyumptious ice cream.

We missed the first round and looking at the leader board, Billy is storming ahead getting 9.2 points from the judges. Luke is in 4th position, with a very well respected 7.2 points. On the replays it shows that the judges have scored Billy high for his innovation and degree of difficulty. Very impressive. He looks like he owns the sea and the surfers around him are insignificant. The power he must feel. Some bloke from Belgium has received a penalty for interfering in Luke's wave. Maybe he could have scored more if he wasn't hindered? Possibly a top 2 place in round one? I was looking forward to watching him perform and wishing him well. I feel so bad that I stayed at his last night with his big competition today. I'm learning how selfish I have actually been and it is not pretty when you discover this truth about yourself.

The radio DJ declares that the next heats are about to start again and the crowd cheer with excitement. I notice Tom is over near the stage chatting to Poppy. This sends a funny feeling to my stomach. I don't want to fall out with him, but he must not chastise me for things his ex has done. He can warn me for sure, but not blame me. That hurt. I continue to dig into my ice cream and look away from my condescending brother. The second round is on its way and Billy Morth takes centre stage again. He is a beast. Everyone is mesmerised looking at the skill and prowess of the Adonis on the big screens. This guy must see some action, the girls are practically panting all around me.

"I met him this morning." I tell Jen. "He is just as miraculous as you would expect, let me tell you. I couldn't move from the sand. He had me cast under some sort of spell. Tom pulled me away, but I can tell that he is dangerous."

"Oh boy, I know what you are like with dangerous men. Practically throw yourself at them." Jen warns.

"I know. I have told myself off for being so pathetic. But just watch him Jen. You don't see men like that here every day."

"Good job or you would be in a constant state of arousal and confusion and I don't have enough in my friendship bag to help you out daily with that." We both begin to giggle, because she is surely right and yes having someone living around here like that would send me back to being a teenager and making more stupid choices than I do now.

"Look, Luke's up." I point over to the action. His face pops up on the screen and I feel a pang of happiness and warmth rise up within me. He really does make me smile.

"Did anything happen last night with him?" Jen asks.

"No, apart from this." I lift my hair to show her the bruise on my head. Jen's eyes widen. "He carried me to his room and banged my head. I sparked out on his bed and he had the couch."

"Firstly, you sparking out is classic for you. Secondly, how did he carry your big arse upstairs? I have a great deal more respect for the poor bloke and he didn't even see any action."

"You cheeky bugger!" I nudge her jokingly.

"Yes he really is a gentleman. We sat and drank tea and put the world to rights. He listened to me blathering on when he should have been resting up for today. I'm an idiot. He is too nice for me."

"I think maybe you would run rings around him and he would let you. He is very handsome – but how does he compare to the love of your life James?"

"Now, there is the million dollar question. I have been comparing them when I shouldn't have. They are both very different. Luke just goes for it and James is very timid and loving. Ideally, I would love to have one night with Billy, Luke and James. Get down to some real nitty gritty – have fun and see who is for me." I laugh but Jen doesn't.

"Em, my lovely friend. Have you not learnt anything from high school? You always said the only way you would find out if you had a connection with a boy was to kiss them. You know from experience that never works out. Now you are in your thirties and you are thinking along the same lines." This comment floors me. She is absolutely right.

"Maybe, it is because I have not really had the chance to experience love with anyone before. Not really sure how I tread forward. Couples make all their mistakes in their twenties and then make relationships work long term. I just do not know how to do that and the longer I am not with anybody – the more I feel it is just not meant to be and I will never experience that."

"You need to remember Em that James is in the same position as you. You will both be unsteady and not know how to move forward. You need to have patience. If anyone of them came over to introduce you to their girlfriend; which one would hurt the most?" Jen asks. I sit and ponder this very good question and go through each scenario in my head. Billy well only met him a few hours ago, he could have seven wives already on the go around the globe. Luke is like another Jen to me. I would love his friendship, but wouldn't feel all that jealous. Then there is James. Makes my inside do Wigfield's Saturday Night every time I see him. I would punch him in the nose if that ever happened and have a total ban on his sausage butties. A real disaster. He is the one, always has been and always will be. I say it out loud.

"James is the one."

"James is the one." I declare again.

"Bloody hell, give the girl a ruddy medal. She has got it." Jen lifts up her tub of ice cream to give me a cheers.

"I am off to get us a nice chilled glass of Champers. This revelation deserves to be remembered!"

Jen stands up and heads off. Leaving me feeling like a weight has been lifted and I put a plan into place to clear this all up.

Chapter
– Sixteen –

The competition has concluded and of course the mighty Billy stormed the heats and rounds. He's leading the WSL quite comfortably and everyone has stayed on the beach to party and celebrate the success of the day. It seems competitors, judges and visitors are always surprised by how good the surf and set up is here. Well, the results from this year's Surf Fest will put us right up there with leading beaches around the world. Very positive for local businesses, my mum will be pleased. The lovely Luke has finished third and he is hot on the heels of the leading two surfers. I just think he needs to have a little more flow on his manoeuvres and he will soon to be on the top podium. Hey, but what do I know? Just what I heard other pros commenting on. I try and listen and pick up the lingo, but I am totally rubbish.

Jen and I head over to a roaring fire pit that has been set up with a temporary bar in an old Citroen van. It looks classic with all the fairy lights dangling around it. A real beach vibe. Most of the surfers are already chilling and chatting about the day, drinking and talking in their alternative language. I excuse myself from Jen and explain that I am heading off to see Luke to clear a few things up. She wishes me luck as I head off, feeling bloody nervous. I am near the changing area searching, when someone whisks me off my feet and twirls me round. Their muscles are rippling around my waste and I can't break free. As I land they spin me round into the chest of Aquaman. Oh dear lord help me and everything within me to cope with this Adonis.

"Emma isn't it?" I just nod.

"Come on girl and celebrate today with me. I'm feeling good, let's down a few beers and feel good together." He grabs my hand and begins to pull me back over to the bar. I begin by walking with him a little confused and taken aback. This shit just keeps on happening. I am living in the land of make believe! "I'm only here one night Emma, let's get crazy." This comment stops me in my tracks. Wake up Emma, he is just like rubber lips – a player. In the words of Grange Hill – just say no! I release my hand and Billy turns around. "What's up baby doll? Want to omit the bar completely? Sure, why not you minx." Billy starts to head towards his hotel.

"No, Billy stop." I shout at the top of my lungs, actually pissed at the cocky nerve of this dude. "As bloody gorgeous and talented as you are. This is not for me. Sorry. I am into someone else." Billy does not look impressed and confused about it. It must have never happened to him before.

"Emma, I'm here." Luke waves and begins to run over.

"You are with the third place geek?" Billy asks in a real condescending tone. I am disliking him the more I am with him. What a prize prick.

"Yes but thanks for the tempting offer." I stick my peacock feathers out and run over to Luke. I quickly turn for a peek and see Billy heading over back to the bar, with two girls already wrapped around him. Good luck to them. Not for me.

As I reach Luke I embrace him, to congratulate him for his result and for being such a nice guy. "Well done today, you were amazing. Gave Billy a run for his money."

"Thanks Emma, so glad you are here now. It's funny I have been really looking forward to seeing you all day." This makes my insides go weak. A man being honest and up front – I love it. He looks so handsome with his bare feet, ripped jeans and pale blue Fistral Beach hoodie. I need to speak with him now, before I fall for this man and the whole situation goes too far.

"Luke, before you head over to celebrate can we have a minute together?" I ask.

"Sure." He holds my hand and we head to sit on a bench which overlooks the bay. It looks stunning and very romantic. Luke obviously feels the same. "Wow, what a spot." He isn't looking at the view, he is looking directly at me. My face beams red and my knees begin to knock. Tell him Emma. I close my eyes, take a deep breath and...I feel soft, succulent lips begin to caress mine. He has taken me by surprise and all my body can do is let my lips do the talking. But they are fully engrossed in this moment and do not utter a single word. This is so arousing, I cannot even come up for air. As he stops he presses his nose to mine. "I have been waiting to do that all night and all day Emma and it was everything I had hoped for." He begins to slowly move in for round two. "That guy over there is beginning to freak me out. He has been watching us the whole time." I look in the direction Luke is pointing and James is stood there looking shell shocked. Oh no, what have I done? Our eyes meet and I can see disgust and hurt in his eyes. This was not my plan at all. Why do I continue to be railroaded and swept along by men I am not really interested in? I have hurt him and that is something I never wanted to do.

"Luke, I'm so sorry. You are utterly amazing and I have never found someone who I can talk to so easily, who is honest and a gentleman. But I am in love with someone else. I have been so caught up in the fact that you like me for me, that I didn't realise that you actually do like me – for real and not in a dream. I am very lucky to have met you, but this moment in time I need to sort this out and let you get on with your life." Luke now looks bewildered and hurt.

"Is it Billy? Everyone falls for Billy. I saw the way he was looking at you." He asks with shakiness in his voice.

"Oh lord no Luke. It is someone who I have known for many years and I have loved for many years, but I have ballsed it up, like I do everything in life and now I need to work my arse off to make it right."

"Is it something I have done or could have done? Tell me I will sort it. I've not met anyone quite like you Emma." Luke looks at me with pleading eyes.

"I am so sorry Luke but no. Any girl would be lucky to have you, but that is not me." I stand up. "I asked you here to tell you that, then our lips locked and I got carried away. I need to go and make things right."

"Thanks for everything Emma, you have made my experience here...memorable." He says with a slight smile on his rejected face. I run to where James left then turn towards Luke.

"Good luck with the rest of the competition and please beat the shit out of 'Billy I am a Knob Morth'." Luke sticks me the thumbs up and with that I leg it to find James. To try and make right, what my stupid head should have done all along.

Chapter
– Seventeen –

Now, if you have some violins could you send them round to mine and help me heal my sorrows. I am sulking under my duvet and going over the previous day in my head – how could I have been such an idiot? After I left Luke I searched the whole ruddy area for James. Not one sight of him. I found my mum, who had no sympathy what so ever for me and told me off for ruining my chance to finally be happy. I saw Tom who also told me what an idiot I had been and then cursed me if I had ruined his chance of going into business with James. I left them both on heated terms and I didn't hear Tom return to my apartment last night, so he must have been well and truly pissed at me. I am not used to being in everyone's dog house, that's for sure and it is an uneasy feeling in my stomach. What a whirlwind the last few days have been. It's gone from men not even noticing me, to four gorgeous hunk of burnin' loves wanting to know me more. I was not prepared and definitely not used to the attention, hence the total feck up on my part. Even my family disowned me, which hurts the damn most.

The weather outside is even cooking up a shit storm and is reflecting my bad, pissed off with myself mood. I can hear the wind pounding against the window giving me a further headache and the rain is sliding down the windows in the same sad way; my tears are on my puffy face. I feel a mess and a certainly look it. The sound of the front door closing makes me jump. Tom must be back. I leap out of bed and run into the kitchen where I find him putting the kettle on, with his back to me.

"Morning." I say tentatively.

"Morning Em." He replies quietly, still in his clothes from the day before.

"Can I have my brother back please? I am beyond sorry if I have messed things up for you." Tom turns and gives me a warm smile.

"Do you want a tea? You look like you could do with it Em. You look shite!" He opens his arms and I run and fling myself in them. "Can't be mad at you for too long. Sorry I was so hard on you. I've made plenty of mistakes in London and I would have been peeved if anyone was judgemental with me."

"It's fine and yes I probably needed a few home truths. Don't think I will ever grow up." I look him up and down.

"Don't be making comments on my appearance when you look bloody rough and smell so bad." Tom sniffs his arm pit and pulls a face in agreement and self-disgust.

"I stayed on Poppy's sofa and before you say anything nothing happened. To the dismay of Poppy, as she tried to entice me into her room several times. She was truly miffed off. I left early on before I could face that scowl she kept giving me. So, we have both pissed off the Dunn family in one night. I can't comment on what's happened to you, because I strung poor Poppy along. It was nice having the attention after cow face Lucy hurt me." I don't say anything. We both take our brews and head into the living room. "Now you know I am also an idiot, tell me the truth about what happened with you Em."

"I just got so caught up with men actually liking me, it was such a wonderful feeling and know this may sound sad but it made me feel lovely and beautiful. As a matter of fact it says more about my low self-esteem than anything now I look at it. I've always had feelings for James and was ready to act on them, but then I met Luke. In my mind Luke was my back-up plan if things didn't work with James. Sounds awful saying this out loud." I take a sip before continuing and Tom just sits and listens. "It's so flattering to have attention, which isn't thrust upon me by our mother. I want those special moments with men like in the romance movies. I want to live in a dream. Sounds crazy? Don't answer that. I know in my heart that James is the one, always has been. I was telling this to Luke last night, but he ended up kissing me. I actually felt nothing, but I wanted that moment. However, as soon as I saw James' distraught face I knew what a missive mistake I had made. It hurts me knowing that I have hurt him. I searched everywhere last night, but couldn't find him."

"Sounds to me Em, that you have done a lot of growing up in a short space of time. I know where James went last night." I turn to Tom, eyes eager for information.

"He spent the night on his boat. I went with Poppy to check on him. He was crazy mad and upset. Cursing you. He told us both to go away and leave him on his own. Poppy said she had never seen James like this about a girl." This information hurts me to hear. "We left him and walked backed to Poppy's. Thought I would bob down this morning and see him."

"Do you think he will still be there?" I ask in hope.

"Not sure with the bad weather, why?"

He didn't need to say anymore. I ran into my bedroom, donned my tracksuit and a rain mac as swiftly as humanly possible. Tom came in looking startled.

"Are you okay? What are you doing Em?"

"To put things right and do something I should have done from the start." With that I give Tom a kiss on his cheek and run outside into the wild weather. "Wish me luck." I shout as I slam the door shut.

Gosh, the wind is pushing against me. Making it a real challenge for me to even get near the boat yard. It is like a ghost town today – boats are bobbing up and down in the greyness, everything is shut and there is a very eerie, uneasy feeling around me. My clothes are stuck to my body and are feeling very heavy soaking up the rainfall. The wind keeps whipping my sodden hair into a frenzy, causing it to stick to my face, making it difficult to see. I sight James' boat, memories of our happy day out flash across my mind. What I'd give to go back in time and do things differently. I climb aboard and shout "James. James are you here?" No reply. I try the door and it opens into the cabin below. There are blankets and a small heater, evident he has spent the night here. I feel the cup of tea – still warm he must be close by. I look around once more before I leave, just encase he is hiding from me. Surely people in real life don't do that kind of thing..do they? I race back on deck and search around. I catch a glimpse of a yellow coat heading to the beach. That must be James, I always make fun of his fisherman's coat. I jump off the boat and run as fast as my little legs can towards him. He's only walking, but he seems faster than me.

"James. Please stop." I shout and pant. I am so unfit. Running on the sand isn't easy at the best of times, but as my trainers have soaked up the ocean it feels like bleeding lead. I stop and launch them into the sea, hoping to give me more speed. "James, James. I am sorry. Please stop." He either can't hear me or he is ignoring me. Something inside me feels it is the latter and this ignites a whole lot of fire and adrenaline in my body. I forget about the pain, about the extra weight of rainfall currently enjoying the ride in my tracksuit. I move at what seems like lightning speed, to catch up with him pure determination to get myself heard. I touch his shoulder and he spins round with balls of fire in his eyes. "James, I'm sorry. I..." He walks away from me and ignores me. I feel sick. I run in front of him in order to stop him in his tracks, but he walks around me.

"Go away Emma. I asked you not to hurt me and that is exactly what you did." He spits at me with venom and hurt. This pisses me off. He is not giving me the chance to tell him that I did balls up. But ironically I didn't give him a chance at all.

"James Dunn. Just stop where the bloody Nora you are standing. I love you. Always have and always will." Waves are starting to batter us, but we both stand still. James is facing away from me, but at least he is listening. "You may have been frightened about getting hurt, well I was too. I was scared if I told you that I loved you it would not be reciprocated. Just by the look on your face, I know you do care for me."

Rain is lashing down my face and I am struggling to talk. James turns to look at me. I walk towards him slowly, in a bid not to scare him off. "I didn't mean to hurt you at all. Thinking deep down I couldn't quite believe that you actually liked me. It's my own fault I should have spoken to you about how I truly felt." James doesn't utter a word. I raise my hand to remove his hood and see his face clearly. My insides are doing a zumba workout at the sight of his beautiful face. I touch his cheek ever so gently and it is a welcome relief to see that he doesn't flinch. "I love you James Dunn. I have wanted to tell you that for many years, but I have never had the guts. Too afraid. Please can you find it in your heart to hear me out properly and forgive me?" He closes his eyes and pushes his face more into the palm of my hand. "When you saw me last night with Luke I was telling him I wasn't interested but he kissed me and that's when you saw us. Please believe me nothing is going on..." James opens his eyes and pulls my face towards his. No words are uttered. The passion that takes over our bodies is undeniable and we kiss each other with neediness, with fire and overall with love and understanding. As we slowly move away our tired, wet lips James holds my hand and simply says "Emma, you are all I have ever wanted. You are beautiful, talented and above all caring. I know you have absolutely no common sense, but I am willing to work on that. I love you too, always have and always will." Tears begin to prick the corners of my eyes. I am finally a leading lady of my own life and this moment has topped all of my movie starred dreams.

One year later

I have just left Tom working in his new premises near the boat yard. He is so happy, now he is living back with his friends and family. Mum keeps turning up with yummy goodies. I think she can't quite believe he is back and wants to keep checking that he hasn't done a runner. He is far away from the painful thoughts of Lucy and it seems to have changed him the whole experience. He has a close friendship with Poppy, but he has put his mind into making the tour business a success with James. Tom mainly does the PR and does a lot of the guided talks on the boat. James and Bobby are the culinary experts and treat visitors to local produce with extraordinary views. It's only been up and running for a few months, but it is bringing more tourists to the area. Dad is trying to get in on the business and develop his kayaking tours.

I head back to my apartment, which has been taken over by James and Tom. I turn up after work to them sat in my spot on the balcony demolishing my wine. I love it.

"James, I'm home." As I enter James' home the music is loud and pounding. It takes me a moment to realise that I can hear James singing to one of my American Anthem tunes. I peek around the kitchen door, to a sight that will be engraved on my mind. James holding the washing up liquid singing to Heart's 'Alone' and scrubbing the dishes with my pinafore on. I lean against the kitchen door frame with goose bumps all over my body. I found my hunk of burnin' love and in the words of Heart 'You don't know how long I've waited.'

Musical References

If you now feel the need to make yourself a mix tape or playlist, the following songs and artists were mentioned in Hunk of Burnin' Love:

The title of my book is linked to Elvis Presley, an artist my brother listened to everyday and now I am an avid fan. I will visit Graceland one day.

Here are all the songs for your enjoyment:

Take my breath away	Berlin
Crazy	Patsy Cline
Shut up and dance	Walk the Moon
She's Electric	Oasis
Baby I don't care	Transvision Vamp
Place you hands	Reef
Would I lie to you	Charles and Eddie
She's a maniac	Michael Sembello
These dreams	Heart – soundtrack of the book

You do something to me	Paul Weller
Wild one	Billy Idol
Frankie (my all time favourite)	Sister Sledge
Nathan Jones	Bananarama
Sweetness	Michelle Gayle
Hearts on fire	John Cafferty
I should be so lucky	Kylie Minogue
Free	Ultra Nate
Freedom	Wham
Let's hear it for the boys	Deniece Williams
More than a feeling	Boston
You've lost that loving feeling	Righteous Brothers
Alone	Heart
Hooked on a Feeling	Blue Suede

Acknowledgements

Writing this book has been an utterly delightful experience. I have made myself giggle and I have used it as a form of escapism from some crazy moments, which life tends to launch at us and smack us straight in the mush. Writing for me is such an enjoyable experience and makes me explore worlds that I dream about or watch in a good old romantic movie.

My family are the most important element of my life and they do daft things everyday to make me smile. I'd like to thank my husband, from the bottom of my pencil case. He is wonderful and supportive and knows I have no common sense at all and still loves me. My son wows me every day with his view on the world and makes life simple again. Just how it should be.

Then there's the Macleod clan; my brother for not taking life too seriously and showing me how to do Shakin' Steven's moves. My mum who listens to me moan everyday and doesn't tell me to shut up. My dad who sadly passed away when I was 18, for introducing me to the world of music. You all make me who am I. Thank you to Michele and Clare, my lovely friends, who have read and chatted with me about the book.

Also to Book Bubble Press for their guidance and knowledge. I just want to thank you all for your constant encouragement and love. This is my first book and fingers crossed I have a couple more in me.

I hope reading it, you most of all find enjoyment and feel the need to head to the sea, have a sausage butty and a good cup of tea!

Catherine Macleod

About the Author

Catherine Macleod is an author from Manchester, England. Her aim is to entertain her readers and ensure they are fully immersed in the lives of the characters she portrays. Catherine wants to bring humour and love to households with her writing.

Thank you for reading her debut book.

If you wish to follow Catherine further, you can find her on Facebook: Write To Entertain or through Book Bubble Press.

@writetoentertain
@bookbubblepress